"*Charity suffereth long, and is kind; charity envieth not; charity vaunteth not itself, is not puffed up, doth not behave itself unseemly, seeketh not her own, is not easily provoked, thinketh no evil; rejoiceth not in iniquity, but rejoiceth in the truth; beareth all things, believeth all things, hopeth all things, endureth all things.*" *The Lord teaches us that in I Corinthians 13, and I certainly committed these verses to memory as a child and carried the words in my heart as if I knew exactly what they meant.*

Today those words pierce my heart and expose my guilt. My tears blur the page as I think of how I misjudged my beloved Jason. How could I have thought the worst of him? How could I have accused him of wrong motives? My love is a weak and poor thing if it proves faithless in the face of doubt; such a love does not come from the One who never gives up on me even when the rest of the world would do so. It is He who shows me the heart of a true friend. How I long to possess that heart!

Prudence Willard
November 4, 1859

SECRETS OF WAYFARERS INN

SECRETS OF
WAYFARERS INN

Before It's Too Late

KATHLEEN Y'BARBO

New York

Secrets of Wayfarers Inn is a trademark of Guideposts.

Published by Guideposts Books & Inspirational Media
110 William Street
New York, NY 10038
Guideposts.org

Cover and interior design by Müllerhaus
Cover illustration by Greg Copeland, represented by Deborah Wolfe, LTD.
Typeset by Aptara, Inc.

Printed and bound in the United States of America
10 9 8 7 6 5 4 3 2 1

SECRETS OF
WAYFARERS INN

Before It's Too Late

CHAPTER ONE

Forget December. November was by far the busiest month of the year.

Janice Eastman absolutely adored the holidays. From the first hint of fall in the air until the last bell was rung at midnight on New Year's Day, she loved every minute of it.

When her husband was living, she would make sure that everything in their home, a lovely parsonage adjacent to the church where he was senior pastor, was decorated just so. That careful attention to detail also made its way into the church where she either hung decorations or supervised their hanging in every nook and cranny of the building.

Thanksgiving decorations ranged from beautiful pumpkins and horns of plenty filled with fall foliage to a quilted banner she sewed herself and hung in the entryway of the parsonage. Close on the heels of the annual city-wide Thanksgiving festivities came the Christmas season, which generally meant clearing out the fall decorations to make way for the celebration of Christ's birth while the pumpkin pie still languished in the fridge.

From beautiful red poinsettias in every room to fragrant greenery draped wherever she could find a place for it, she never failed to create a festive atmosphere. Now that she was a widow, and a lovely young couple had taken up residence in the parsonage, Janice translated that affinity for the holidays to other outlets—and other beneficiaries, namely her best friends Tess Wallace and LuAnn Sherrill.

Though the trio had owned Wayfarers Inn for only a short time, Janice found it difficult to recall most of what life was like prior to moving to the inn's top floor. Some of it she couldn't help but recall. Losing her husband and finding a void that had been impossible to fill was the one memory that would never fade. Moving in with her daughter and searching for what God wanted as she faced widowhood was another.

Oh, but God had blessed her so wonderfully with friends and a purpose, even though that void where her husband used to be would never be filled completely. Last year her grief had been too fresh, but this year she determined to at least begin a very special banner to honor the holidays. Made from her husband's Christmas ties, the quilted banner would not only brighten up the inn's lobby, but it would also bring a little of the past into the present.

But first she had to get through Thanksgiving.

She lifted her attention from the ancient *Betty Crocker Cookbook* on the counter in front of her to watch Winnie Washington, the inn's cook, effortlessly stirring the three simmering pots in front of her. Standing in front of Big Red, the inn's massive antique red stove, Winnie looked like a conductor directing an orchestra. First the saucepan, then the soup pot, then back to the frying pan she went, her strong arms never pausing.

"Janice, you're woolgathering again," Winnie said before turning to face her. "What's the matter?"

The question flustered her. "Nothing and everything," she finally admitted.

Winnie swiveled to adjust the knobs on the stove and then moved over to pour two cups of coffee. She perched on a stool opposite Janice and slid one of the mugs toward her.

"All right," she said to Janice. "Spill. And I don't mean the coffee."

Janice smiled in spite of herself. "How is it you always know such things, Winnie?"

Her friend shrugged and took a sip of coffee. "You're stalling. Something wrong?"

"I'm just tired," she said. "Busy. Maybe a little overwhelmed."

Winnie just sat quietly and sipped her coffee while the delicious scents from the stove swirled around them. Janice gathered her thoughts and then picked up her mug.

"What happened to the days when we had Thanksgiving before Christmas?" she mused. "I love celebrating Christmas as much as the next person, but the decorating committee had us out hanging tinsel and lights in downtown Marietta before the end of October this year. And the Christmas parade is two days after Thanksgiving. We won't even be rid of the leftover turkey by then."

"I agree," Winnie said, her voice soft and silky against the quiet of the morning. "They do tend to rush things nowadays, but that's not limited to the holidays." She paused. "Is that all that's bothering you today?"

Janice glanced one more time at the cookbook, now open to a chocolate cake recipe that she could recite by heart after more than forty years of making it. She closed the book and traced the ragged edge of the red-checked cover with her index finger.

"Can't we just slow down?" Janice met Winnie's comforting look. "I know we can't, not really, but what's the harm in trying?"

"No harm at all," Winne said. "Unless you happen to own an inn that is busy for the entire month and has a waiting list the week of Thanksgiving. And don't forget we are also contributing to the city-wide meal this year."

"And entering a float in the Christmas parade," Janice said.

"The one you just said is two days after Thanksgiving?"

"Yep." At the sight of Winnie's wide eyes and open mouth, Janice said, "I guess I haven't mentioned that part, have I?"

"No," Winnie said. "I would remember if you had."

"It'll be a simple float just like we did for the Fourth of July parade before the inn opened. Since Tess's son's truck is red, it'll be the perfect parade float. That is, if he agrees to it. If he doesn't, we could ask about the antique firetruck if the fire department isn't using it. We can use the Christmas quilt we'll drape over the upstairs railing to go on whichever truck we have, and we'll put a big wreath with a red bow on the front. No fuss, and it will be adorable."

The kitchen door burst open, and Tess hurried inside. LuAnn followed on her heels. Both went straight for the coffeepot.

"What will be adorable?" Tess asked as she set two mugs on the counter and then stepped back to allow LuAnn to pour.

"Oh, we're just talking about the inn's float in the Marietta Christmas parade," Winnie said with a grin.

"We're entering a float in the parade?" LuAnn said. "I had no idea."

"Neither did I," Tess said, "but it sounds like fun."

"I'm sorry," Janice said as her best friends joined them at the table. "It all happened while we were working on the decorations for downtown a couple of weeks ago. I told you I couldn't be trusted to attend a Christmas event so early in the season. I get way too enthusiastic."

LuAnn reached over to pat Janice on the arm. "There is nothing wrong with enthusiasm. Exactly what have you—or rather we—committed to?"

"Just a float in the parade," she said. "I thought we could keep it simple and do something similar to last year's Fourth of July parade only swap the red, white, and blue quilt for a red and green one, that is if Jeff Jr. wouldn't mind us dragging him in to participate. Put a wreath on the front, and his truck is a Christmas parade float."

"With one big difference," Tess said. "Instead of melting into a puddle in the July heat, the three of us will be freezing in the back."

"That's true," Janice said. "I don't suppose it's too late to pull out."

"No," LuAnn and Tess said in unison.

"Then it's settled," LuAnn said as she opened her ever-present notebook and reached for her pen. "We'll do the parade. And if it's too cold, we'll just dress up in something warm enough to get us all the way down Main Street without turning into Popsicles."

"Oh we'll all be Popsicles when we're done, I guarantee," Tess said, "but it'll still be fun. I wouldn't miss it for the world."

"Well, you can count me out," Winnie said. "I will be far too busy back here at the inn keeping the soup and wassail warm so my Popsicles can come home and thaw out."

"Thank you, Winnie," Janice said. "We'll be ready for something warm, that's for sure."

"So when is the parade exactly?" LuAnn said, her pen poised to write the information on her calendar.

"The Saturday morning after Thanksgiving," Janice told them.

"What?" LuAnn said. "Two weeks from today?"

"It won't even be December," Tess added. "What's the rush?"

Janice shrugged. "Exactly what Winnie and I were just talking about. Next thing you know we'll go straight from Fourth of July fireworks to trim-the-tree without blinking."

"Well, I don't like it," Tess declared.

"But what can you do about it?" Winnie said.

Janice grinned as a thought occurred. "I know what I'm going to do about it. I am going to declare this month a Thanksgiving-only month." She shrugged. "Okay, except for what we absolutely have to do to get ready for the parade."

"And the Christmas decorations for the inn," LuAnn reminded her. "Our guests will expect it."

"Our guests can wait until the first day of December," Tess said. "I think Janice is onto something here. We rush through a day of giving thanks in order to get to a season where we wear ourselves out giving gifts. I think we need to be intentional about doing something different this year."

"Like what?" LuAnn said.

Both women looked to Janice as if she had the answer. Her phone rang, giving her a brief reprieve. She pulled her phone from her pocket and saw her son's name.

"It's Stuart. I should get this. But I agree with everything you've said." She looked at the clock above the sink. "Stuart, what's wrong?"

"Nothing is wrong. Why?"

"It's the middle of the morning. Shouldn't you be at work?"

He laughed. "I am at work. But I had a little break, and I wanted to give you a call."

"Who died?"

"Mom, no one died. This is good news."

"Good news?" Janice was hesitant. "What is it?"

"Ma" he said quietly. "Are you sitting down?"

CHAPTER TWO

November 2, 1859

The infant was lovely. Though matted, her dark hair shone in the morning sun. When Prudence came upon the blanketed bundle, curled up among the leaves in a gown of white cotton with lace trim, she thought she'd nearly stumbled over an angel unaware. Then that angel opened dark eyes and let out a cry.

"Oh, honey," Prudence said as she scooped the little one into her arms. The child was newly born and weighed almost nothing when compared to her sturdy son, Moses. "Surely thee is not out here all alone."

The November wind rustled the trees, and the little one shuddered. Prudence opened her shawl and tucked the squirming bundle close against her. Instantly the baby quieted.

"Where is thy mama and daddy, little one?" she asked as she glanced around.

Though this child did not look to be one of the many who escaped slavery to land on this side of the Ohio River, Prudence knew all too well that looks could be deceiving. She had helped enough travelers along the Underground Railroad to realize that the color of a baby's skin did not define whether that child was slave or free.

In times like these, danger always lurked just close enough to be ever mindful of it. Keeping her attention on the trail, she moved as silently as she could toward the river in the hopes that the little one's family would be nearby. When she saw no evidence of others having arrived during the night, Prudence turned back toward home.

For though she had no idea what to do with this child, she did know how to care for a baby. And this baby was hungry and needed a fresh set of clothes.

These things she could provide until the child's mama was found.

CHAPTER THREE

E ngaged?" Tess and LuAnn squealed in unison.

"That's what he said." Janice's grin quickly shifted to a giggle and then bubbled up as laughter. "He called me because he was hoping to use my mother's engagement ring. Isn't that just beautiful? Mom would be so happy."

"That is such a lovely idea," LuAnn said.

"Yeah, and it saves him a ton of money to boot," Tess said with a smile. "Not that that's what he was thinking about, of course."

"Stuart did inherit his father's frugality," Janice said. "But as long as Zelda doesn't mind, I'm all for it. I love the idea of passing down a family heirloom. It's a lovely ruby surrounded by tiny diamonds, and it's just sitting in my jewelry box."

"It sounds beautiful," LuAnn said.

"But mum's the word until Zelda says yes." Janice clapped her hands together. "But, oh my goodness, my boy is finally getting married."

"Now that is the best thing I've heard all day," Winnie said.

"So when is he going to ask her, and when will the wedding be?" LuAnn turned to the calendar on the kitchen wall.

Janice shrugged. "He didn't say, but knowing Stuart, he won't wait long. He said he's eager to make her his bride."

Stuart had already waited a long time, after all. He'd dated Zelda McLoughlin in high school and never quite gotten over her. When they'd reunited earlier this year, he had fallen hard for her again, and even though Zelda spent much of her time traveling as part of a Christian band, they talked every day. And Zelda's nineteen-year-old daughter, Brin, seemed to be very happy for her mother.

Tess shook her head. "If Zelda wants a big wedding, he may have to be patient."

"Yes, she might, and that would be just as wonderful as if they decided on a small wedding." Janice couldn't contain another giggle. "Oh, ladies, I am so happy for them. And I get a new granddaughter too. Brin is such a lovely young lady."

There was a time, briefly, when Janice suspected that Stuart might have been the teenager's father. He wasn't, but now he would get to be her stepfather.

"I hope he hurries," Tess said. "I don't see how you're going to keep this secret from Zelda."

"Oh." Janice's elation turned to worry. "Zelda. She's heading up the committee for the Thanksgiving Feast. She's in charge now that Bev Thornton has broken her back and can't do the job."

As a pastor's wife, Janice had participated in the annual city-wide Thanksgiving celebration for as long as she could remember, except last year, when the inn had been newly opened, and there just hadn't been time. It was a unique event, and one that blessed many people in Marietta. The premise was simple—everyone in town was invited to celebrate Thanksgiving together at Christ Fellowship Church. They pushed the pews against the walls, set up tables, and ate together. Of course not everyone attended, as many people chose to celebrate at home with their families, but the planning committee made sure that everyone who wanted to participate was able to. There were even deliveries for those who couldn't attend in person, with an elaborate volunteer army driving meals all over town. There were plenty of people who wouldn't have a Thanksgiving meal without the committee's work, and the annual event was one of Janice's favorites.

"It was very kind of her to take over for Bev with less than three weeks to go before the event," LuAnn said. "Especially since she's preparing for a tour in the spring. Between rehearsing, spending time with Brin, and hosting that young singer, she must already have her hands full."

Stuart had mentioned that Zelda had taken in Ellen Randall, a twenty-year-old singer with a bright future ahead but an awful home life behind her, on the request of the music agent they shared. He hoped Zelda and Brin would keep Ellen out of trouble during the down time between concerts. When Janice expressed concern, Stuart assured her that Ellen just needed to be shown there was a better way to live than the life she came from.

"Oh, Zelda is absolutely wonderful, and I know she'll be a great example to Ellen," Janice said. "But I'll have to be very careful around Zelda at the meeting. I would hate to let something slip and ruin it for them."

Tess wrapped her arm around Janice's shoulder. "You'll do fine. You will simply talk about the food and the event, and you will pretend you did not have a conversation with your son this morning that had anything to do with Zelda or rings or proposing."

"Take one of these two with you," Winnie said. "They'll keep you out of trouble." Then she shook her head and laughed. "What am I saying? The three of you always manage to find trouble."

LuAnn grinned. "I think trouble always finds us."

"If it will make you feel better, I'll go with you," Tess said to Janice. "I was hoping to volunteer for the event anyway. And I can keep you out of trouble."

Janice sighed. "Thank you, Tess. That would be wonderful."

———————

Several hours later the pair walked into Christ Fellowship Church and easily found the Sunday School classroom where the members of the committee had gathered. Zelda had already called the meeting to order, so Janice and Tess slipped inside and took seats in the back row.

Zelda spied them and waved. Janice waved back with a smile as she studied her future daughter-in-law. Dressed in slim-fitting jeans, black boots, and an oversized black sweater, she wore her mahogany-colored hair in a riot of curls that fell to her shoulders. Silver hoop earrings peeked out through the curls and caught the light. It was easy to see how Stuart had fallen in love with her. Not only did Zelda mesmerize fans in her concerts, but she also had everyone in this room paying rapt attention.

"First, thank you all for allowing me to take on this job," she said with a smile. "Marietta was once home to me, and I'm so happy that it is again. Taking over the Thanksgiving Feast committee chair is an honor."

"Let's see how you feel when it's all over," local historian Margaret Ashworth called from the middle of the room.

Janice knew that Margaret had headed the committee for ten years and just this year had passed the responsibility on to Bev Thornton.

Zelda joined the others in laughing. "I'm already beginning to see it's a lot of work. Thanksgiving is less than two weeks away, and we still have so much to do. But before we go any further, could we pray?" She looked to the back of the room. "Janice, would you do the honors?"

Janice happily rose to the occasion as her nerves calmed. She had been worried about speaking to Zelda, but speaking to the Lord was easy. After asking for God's blessing on this meeting and the event, she added a prayer for quick healing for Beverly Thornton. After a hearty amen from all in attendance, Zelda offered a broad smile.

"Just one more thing. I would like to introduce someone very special. Ellen Randall is an amazing singer and an all-around nice person. I am very happy that she will be staying with Brin and me until she—Ellen, that is—and I leave to go on tour in the spring. You're going to love her. Ellen, would you please stand up and say hi?"

After a moment of coaxing, a young woman of approximately Zelda's height and build rose. She wore a baggy University of Hawaii hooded sweatshirt over a pair of torn and faded jeans. Her long dark hair was twisted into a messy bun, and she wore neither jewelry nor makeup. After a quick wave, Ellen hurried to sit back down.

"Ellen will be here until spring tour kicks off, so look for her around town, and be sure to say hello," Zelda added before she got down to business. She asked for updates from each of the members of the committee and then reached for the basket beside her.

"All that remains is to turn in the donations for the event. I understand that this is also the time of year we have our big drive for the food pantry, so if you've collected any funds for that, just be sure they're marked separately from the event funds."

She passed a basket around the room, and everyone put in the donations they'd collected from local businesses as well as neighbors and friends over the past few weeks. Janice's batch of donations included a contribution from Wayfarers Inn as well as checks from the Sassy Seamstress, Jasmine Tea Shop, Antoinette's Closet, McHappy's Donuts, and Morrison's Book Shop. There were also personal donations from each of the innkeepers and several of their neighbors in the stack of bills that Janice placed in the basket. Once the basket had gone around the room, Zelda picked it up and placed it on the table beside her.

"Thank you for your generosity and hard work," Zelda said. "The donations you collected will ensure that everyone in town will get a hot meal to celebrate Thanksgiving, no matter what their circumstances are."

Janice was pleased to see that it looked like they had collected quite a tidy sum. As the basket had gone past her, she'd seen many fifties and hundred-dollar bills mixed in with the checks. She guessed there was several thousand dollars in the basket not including the checks. She felt a surge of pride to be part of such a caring community.

Zelda adjourned the meeting, and as the attendees rose and milled around, Janice watched her empty the contents of the basket into a black bank bag. The bag was so full she had to yank on the zipper to get it closed, then she put it into her purse. She walked over to where Janice and Tess were waiting.

"I'm glad you're here," she said to them. "I was so nervous."

"You?" Tess said. "No way. You're a natural up there on stage."

Zelda shook her head. "Singing, yes, but speaking? No way."

"Maybe you can just sing the next meeting, then," Janice said. She smiled and reminded herself not to say anything about Stuart, or rings, or weddings, or—

"How's it going in the studio?" Tess said, giving Janice a significant look. Thank goodness for Tess, rescuing Janice from herself.

"It's good," Zelda said. "I'm working on what will be my first solo album. It's pretty exciting. I'm having Ellen sing a duet with me for one of the tracks. She's a great songwriter, and our voices blend really well. And we're getting ready for our tour in the spring. We'll be performing at some music festivals and churches, mainly—not selling out arenas yet—but it'll be fun, and hopefully people will show up." She hitched up her purse.

Janice opened her mouth to tell her to keep May and June free because they were the best time for weddings, but Tess jumped in.

"We should probably let Zelda get going," she said as she tugged on Janice's arm. "And we need to get back to the inn." She nodded toward Ellen, who was the sole attendee still seated. "And Ellen probably wants to get out of this room full of old people."

Zelda looked over her shoulder in Ellen's direction then back at Janice and Tess. "She's just shy around people she doesn't know. You'll love her once you get to know her."

"How's she doing? Is she settling in?" Janice asked. Ellen had a sullen expression on her face, and her arms were crossed over her chest.

"She's doing all right." Zelda bit her lip and looked as if she wanted to say more. They waited, and she continued. "Ellen is very private and doesn't say much. I'm hoping she'll warm up to us as she gets used to living here. I know it's just a temporary arrangement until we go on tour in the spring, but I'd still like to see her make herself at home with us."

"I'm sure she will soon," Tess said. "Please let her know she's welcome at the inn anytime she wants to stop in. Free bowl of soup at the café courtesy of the innkeepers."

"That's really kind. I'll make sure she knows," Zelda said.

"You're a good mom and a wonderful example to any young girl," Janice said. "She'll be just fine with you."

Her future daughter-in-law beamed. "Do you think so? I certainly am thankful for this opportunity. Despite our challenges, God has given Brin and me so much. I would love to share that with Ellen, but she thinks that if God really loved her she would be rich and famous and not have to depend on others." Zelda's laugh held no humor. "If that were true, I'd be a doubter too."

"Why would you say that?" Janice asked. "You've got a beautiful daughter, prospects for a career, and a…" She caught herself before she said *fiancé*. "That is, you have Stuart."

"All wonderful things, especially Stuart," Zelda said with a quick smile in Janice's direction. "It's fine. It's just that getting a foothold in a music career is expensive, what with the studio time and promotion fees and everything that goes into an album. And then of course there's rent and groceries for the three of us. It sure adds up." She shrugged. "Hopefully we'll make enough on the tour in the spring to cover the expenses, but in the short term, things are just a bit tight."

"Oh, honey," Janice said. "I'm so sorry. I had no idea. I just assumed…"

"We'll be all right," Zelda said. "We're singing for God's glory, so I have to believe that He's going to take care of us."

"He will," Janice said. "I just know He will."

And it didn't hurt that Stuart made a good salary as a doctor, Janice thought. Once they were married, they'd have Stuart's income to help out.

"I'm sorry to unload on you like that," Zelda said, her expression contrite. "I don't usually talk about the financial side of things."

"That's quite all right," Tess said. "It's on your mind, of course. Especially with all this going on." She gestured around the room, and Janice knew she meant the Thanksgiving event.

Zelda gave them a grateful smile and then called over her shoulder. "Ellen, come and meet my friends."

The young woman gave her a sullen look but stood up. After taking her time to gather her backpack and move across the room, she joined them.

"These are my friends Janice and Tess. They're the owners of Wayfarers Inn, along with their friend LuAnn. Ladies, this is Ellen Randall." She looked at Ellen. "They've told me you're welcome anytime at the inn, and you'll be their guest for soup at the café."

Ellen never met Janice's gaze but mumbled "thanks" under her breath. With her hands stuffed in her pockets, the young singer looked more like a shy teenager than a Christian artist with a successful career ahead of her.

"I'll go wait in the car," Ellen told Zelda.

Zelda replaced what appeared to be a disappointed look with a smile. "Yes, that's fine. You'll need the keys though." She dug around in her purse and finally pulled out the keys attached to a sparkly key chain.

After Ellen disappeared outside, Tess spoke up. "Is she always like that, or was it us?"

"It definitely wasn't you," Zelda said. "Ellen is amazing on stage, and she's got a voice like an angel, but she's also got a long way to go in learning how to trust people. She's suspicious of anyone she doesn't know. She's a challenge, but she'll warm up to you, I promise."

Tess shrugged. "Well, our offer for soup at the café still stands."

"Yes, that's right," Janice said. "And please, let me know if I can be of any help. Between being a mother, a pastor's wife, and a teacher, I've had plenty of experience with challenging people."

Zelda laughed. "Stuart did mention that he and Stacy were quite a handful as children."

"They still are on occasion," she said. "But I wouldn't have it any other way."

Zelda tapped her purse. "All right. I've got to swing by the bank and deposit this, and then I have to tackle the pile of paperwork I've been avoiding."

"Say hi to Brin for us," Janice said. *My soon-to-be granddaughter,* she added in her head.

"I will, if I see her. Now that I'm back in town for a while, she's started taking classes at Marietta College. She got a scholarship," Zelda said with obvious pride on her face. "I'm so proud of her for that. I'd never be able to send her to such a good school otherwise. But she's so busy I almost never get to see her."

"That's hard," Janice said.

"But it's great that she's studying so hard," Tess added. "And about the scholarship."

"You're right about that, Tess." Zelda waved, but Janice couldn't stop herself. She reached over to hug Stuart's future fiancée. Tess did the same, and then she ushered Janice out of the classroom and down the hall toward the exit.

Janice climbed into the car and reached for the seat belt as Tess settled behind the steering wheel. Once the doors were locked and the engine hummed to life, Janice finally let out the breath she was holding. "I wanted to say something about Stuart so badly."

"But you didn't, and that's what matters," Tess said. "When is he going to ask her?"

"I don't know."

"Well, tell him he has to hurry."

Janice pulled the phone out of her purse and found Stuart's number. She put her phone to her ear as Tess pulled out of the parking lot and headed toward home.

"You have got to ask that woman to marry you immediately," Janice said when Stuart answered.

"Hello, Ma," was his calm response.

"Stuart, I just spent an hour at a Thanksgiving Feast planning meeting with Zelda. There's another meeting in a week. If you don't ask her before then, I'm just going to have to skip the meeting. And if I see her before then, well, just pray that I don't, because I'm terrible at keeping a secret, so I'll either have to hide from her or give away your plans."

"Ma," he said gently, "you don't know my plans."

"Well, that's true," she admitted.

"And I don't plan to tell you what they are, so don't worry." He paused. "But if it makes you feel better, I'd like to come by and get the ring this week. I don't have any patients until ten on Wednesday. Could I stop by that morning? Because I do plan to ask Zelda very soon."

"Of course. I'll have it ready." And then, "How soon?"

"I'm not going to tell you," he said. "Just trust me. You won't have to hide for long."

CHAPTER FOUR

After a busy morning seeing to the guests and helping Winnie in the kitchen, Janice wandered back up to the apartment she shared with Tess and LuAnn on the top floor of the inn. LuAnn had stayed to help Winnie get lunch ready, and Tess was working on the laundry. Janice needed to turn over a couple of the suites before more guests checked in, but there was something she needed to do first. She went into her bedroom and opened the jewelry box that had once belonged to her grandmother. The box was made of inlaid walnut in a beautiful flower design, and the box was lacquered to a high shine. Inside, the necklaces and bracelets and rings she'd collected over the years were lined up along the red velvet lining. There it was. Tucked into the tufted ring rows, right next to Janice's own engagement ring, which was no more than a chip of a diamond. Janice lifted her mother's ring and held it up to the light. It was stunning, with a bright oval-shaped ruby surrounded by a ring of tiny diamonds. It needed a good polish, but it would look beautiful on Zelda's finger.

Janice smiled when her phone played James Taylor's "You've Got a Friend." Tess or LuAnn must be calling from downstairs. Janice didn't have a ring box, so she slipped the ring into a small velvet pouch that had held potpourri and dashed to her sitting room where she'd put her phone down.

"Hey," she said, dropping into her armchair.

"Hi, Janice," Tess said. "Can you come down here for a moment? Zelda is here."

Zelda? "I'll be right down."

Janice went back into her bedroom and tucked the pouch into her top drawer carefully. It wouldn't do to lose track of that, she thought as she headed down the stairs.

She found Zelda sitting with Tess on the couch in the lobby. Her face was pale, and the skin around her eyes was puffy. She'd been crying. Oh dear. Had something happened with Stuart?

"Hi, Janice." Zelda tried to smile, but more tears leaked out of her eyes. Tess pulled a tissue from the box on the side table and handed it to her.

"It's going to be okay," Tess said soothingly.

"What's going on?" Janice lowered herself into the chair across from them. She prayed Stuart hadn't done something to upset Zelda.

"I was hoping you guys could walk me through something, to make sure I'm not crazy," Zelda said.

"Of course you're not," Janice said. She glanced at Tess, who shook her head. "What happened?"

"When I was talking to you guys after the meeting on Saturday, do you remember seeing the bank bag with the donations for the Thanksgiving Feast and food pantry in it?"

Janice's heart sank. This could not be good. She thought back for a moment, replaying the conversation in her head, and then she nodded.

"Yes, I remember seeing it. You tucked it into your purse." And then, a beat later, "Why?"

Tears welled up in Zelda's eyes again. "I'm trying to retrace all my steps from that day. I was sure I had the money when I was talking with you. I went straight home before going to the bank because I remembered I had a check I needed to deposit. Then while I was at home I got a phone call from my manager, and we talked for a while about how things are going in the studio and about the tour in the fall, and about Ellen. I guess it ended up being a longer conversation than I expected. I'm sure the bag was still in my purse, because where else would it be? And then I drove straight to the bank. But of course, it was Saturday, and the bank was closed, so I used the night deposit box. I know I did."

Janice knew the deposit box Zelda was talking about because she'd used it herself many times. Several other businesses in town also used it, because it was supposed to be quicker and safer than using an ATM. She held out her hands, palms up. "What could possibly go wrong? You put your deposit into a bank bag with the deposit slip, you put the bag in the slot, and you're done." She shrugged. "It's not rocket science."

"I know, right?" said Zelda.

"Hang on." Tess held up her hand. "Back up. What's going on? Why are you trying to retrace your steps?"

"Because the money is gone," Zelda said. "The bank says I never deposited it, but I know I did."

"*All* of the money is gone?" Janice tried to keep her voice calm, but wasn't sure she succeeded. "Everything we collected for the town Thanksgiving celebration?"

"Yes." Zelda nodded. "According to the bank, they never received it. It seems to have just vanished."

Janice sat back and tried to take this in. There had been several thousand dollars just in the donations she'd collected herself. There had to have been many times that in that envelope.

"It can't have just vanished," Tess said. "That bag has to be somewhere."

"I know." Zelda fisted the tissue. "I agree. But I have no idea where. So, like I said, I'm trying to retrace my steps to try to figure out if there's any possibility I might have lost it along the way. I'm sure I made that deposit, but the bank says I didn't, so I don't know what else to do."

"It can't be that hard to know whether you made the deposit or not," Janice said. "Surely they have security cameras. We'll just ask them to review the footage. That will prove that you made the deposit."

"I already asked about that, and they said the camera over the night deposit box was vandalized Friday, so it wasn't working."

"What?" Tess sounded as indignant as Janice felt. "How can they say that you didn't make the deposit if they can't prove that you didn't?"

Zelda shrugged. "And I've already written several checks to vendors for the meal, so now those checks are going to bounce."

"Oh dear." Janice's stomach was turning. "And there are usually hefty fines for bouncing a check."

"Yes, but the bigger problem is that if I don't find that money, there won't be a town Thanksgiving meal this year," Zelda said. She used the tissue to dab at her eyes again.

"We won't let that happen," Janice promised. "If you say you made that deposit, we believe you. We'll figure out what happened to the money."

Tess was nodding. "That's right. Really, it can't be that hard to track it down. We'll find it."

"Thank you," Zelda said. "For being willing to help, but also for believing me. I thought I was going crazy there for a while."

"Of course we believe you," Janice said. "If you didn't deposit the money, what's the alternative? That you took the money yourself? That's ridiculous." She waved her hand dismissively. "You're a Christian singer, for goodness' sake. Of course you aren't going to steal money that would be used to feed hungry people at Thanksgiving. Let's make a list of all the possibilities, and we can start investigating and figure out where that money went."

"Let me go get LuAnn," Tess said, pushing herself up. "She'll want to be a part of this too."

A few minutes later, LuAnn was seated across from Zelda and had a notebook in her lap.

"Okay, so after you left the meeting at the church, you went straight home?" LuAnn had her pen poised over the blank page.

"Well, not *straight* home. I made a stop at the Better Batter. After that meeting, I needed a treat."

Janice could understand that. Everything Sandie Ballard sold at her bakery was delicious.

"And Ellen wanted to stop at that clothing store in town, the one with the outrageous prices for T-shirts and things?"

"Oh, right." LuAnn was nodding. "What's it called? Fig?"

"Olive," Zelda said. "I'd never been in there, but Ellen apparently had, and she wanted to get a new outfit for a show we're doing at a church in Columbus in a few weeks."

"Right. You had Ellen with you." Janice met Tess's eye. Ellen hadn't struck Janice as particularly trustworthy.

"Yes, but she didn't take the money. Why would she do that?"

Janice could think of one very big reason she could have taken the money—Zelda had already told them how expensive it could be getting a recording career off the ground. And if she was shopping at Olive, she obviously didn't have cheap taste. Janice had never understood how they could charge the prices they did, but apparently enough people were willing to pay it that they stayed in business.

"Did you have your purse with you at each of these stops?" LuAnn asked.

"Yes." Zelda nodded. "I took it in with me, and I'm sure the bank bag was in it."

They'd double-check that by talking to the people at the stores to see if they remembered seeing the bag.

"And then you went home and talked to your manager?" Tess asked.

"That's right."

"And where was the money then?" Janice asked.

"It was in my purse, on a chair by the door."

"Was Ellen home with you?" LuAnn was writing on her notepad.

"Yes. She was there the whole time."

"Anyone else?" Tess asked.

"Brin was there too, for part of it anyway. She was in her room studying when we came home, but she went out before I left for the bank."

"Could you see your purse the whole time?" LuAnn asked.

"No. I was at the kitchen table, and my purse was by the door. You can't see it from there. But there's no way either one of them took the money."

Janice knew that Zelda didn't want to believe that either her daughter or the singer in her care would have taken the money. But with many thousands of dollars at stake, they couldn't afford to ignore any possibilities.

"And when you went to the bank to deposit the money?" Tess asked. "What time was this?"

"It was around four," Zelda said.

"Did anyone go with you?" Janice asked.

"Yes, Ellen went with me," Zelda said. "She says she remembers seeing me make the deposit. But that doesn't help if the bank says I didn't."

"You said you used the night deposit box," Tess said. "When did you fill out the deposit slip?"

"As soon as I got home I took the money out of the bank bag, counted it, and filled out the deposit slip," Zelda said. "Then I put the bag in my purse and put it on a chair by the front door. The deposit slip was in the bank bag."

"And after you made the deposit, you went home?" Tess asked.

"Exactly." Zelda thought for a minute. "Wait—I stopped at Over the Moon first to get a pizza for dinner. But after that, yes, straight home."

"And when did you realize the money hadn't been deposited?" LuAnn asked.

"I went to make a withdrawal this morning," Zelda said. "The florist wanted the deposit in cash, so I used the ATM. After I withdrew the money I checked the balance of the account, and it was nowhere near what it should be. So I went inside, and Paul Townsend told me there was no deposit made over the weekend." She shrugged. "So here I am, trying to make sure I'm not crazy."

"You're not crazy," Janice said. But she hated that this had happened, especially to Zelda, especially right now, when any day Stuart was—but she needed to focus. She had to make sure she didn't blurt that out.

"And we all know how important it is to find that money," Tess said. "Without it, there won't be a Thanksgiving Feast this year."

"We can't let that happen," Janice said.

"Well, there's just one solution," LuAnn said. "We'll just have to find that money."

CHAPTER FIVE

Zelda left, and LuAnn and Tess headed up to the fourth floor. After checking out one of their guests, Janice joined them. They had a few minutes before they needed to help with lunch, and she wanted to regroup privately. Janice smiled as she stepped out of the elevator and into the bright and open apartment the friends shared. While the public spaces at Wayfarers Inn were decorated with themes in keeping with the inn's history, this area had been designed by the innkeepers as a sunny retreat from the busyness downstairs.

The entire apartment consisted of a beautifully furnished living area with a small kitchenette where an electric teapot always stood at the ready. Each of the women had her own suite of rooms consisting of a bedroom, bathroom, and a sitting area. When Janice came in, LuAnn sat writing in her notebook at the table, and Tess was on the couch with both the dog and the cat in her lap.

"Are you two hiding out up here?" Janice said as she closed the door behind her.

"No, we're very busy," Tess said with a grin. "LuAnn is busy making a list of suspects who might have taken the money from Zelda's purse. And I am busy..." She laughed as Huck growled and stretched out as if trying to push Tom off her lap. "Busy playing referee with these two rascals." Tom purred and batted at Huck lazily.

"Great." Janice poured steaming water from the electric kettle over an Earl Grey tea bag and made her way to the chair across from Tess, setting her mug on the coffee table.

"Do you really think we need to think about suspects?" Janice said. "Surely this is all a misunderstanding. Who would steal money from the town's Thanksgiving Feast?"

"I can think of a few people who wouldn't mind a few thousand extra dollars," Tess said. "Ellen, for one. And she had the opportunity while the money was in Zelda's purse at home."

"And Brin also had the same opportunity," LuAnn said.

"Yeah, but what motive would she have?" Janice asked. Brin was such a sweet young woman. *And* her future step-granddaughter.

"Helping her mother with their financial issues?" LuAnn asked.

"Or, wait. Didn't Zelda say she's in college?" Tess asked. "Even if her mother doesn't have the money, and Brin qualifies for scholarships, having a little extra to help pay for next semester's expenses might be on her mind at this point in November."

LuAnn nodded. "I don't know if you've looked at the price of college recently, but I would have to rob a bank to be able to afford it."

Janice looked at Tess, unsure how to respond.

"Anyway, I'm going to mark Brin down for both motive and opportunity," LuAnn said.

"But Zelda said she put the bag in the night deposit slot, right?" Janice said. The other two nodded. "Well, don't you think she would have noticed if the money wasn't in it when she deposited it?"

"Either Ellen or Brin could have taken the cash and checks out and put some other paper inside the bag so she wouldn't notice," Tess said.

"And then there's…" LuAnn's voice trailed off.

Tess glanced nervously at Janice.

"Who?" Janice asked.

"Well, then there's Zelda herself." Tess didn't meet Janice's eyes.

"You think she stole the money?" Janice couldn't believe it. "And just pretended to have deposited it? Why would she do that? She's the one who's responsible for the whole town celebration."

There was a pause that was just a second too long, and then Tess said, "We're not saying she did it, Janice. Just that, well, if we're looking at people who had the opportunity to take the money…"

"Why would she steal the money she was responsible for?" Janice couldn't believe they were even discussing this. "And then go to the bank and try to take the money out and act surprised that it was missing?"

"People have done stranger things to cover up their actions," LuAnn said.

"Again, we're not saying she did it," Tess said. "But, well, you heard her talking about how expensive it is to become a recording artist. It sure sounded like she could use some cash to get her through this time."

"She had nothing to do with it," Janice said. "Aren't we supposed to be helping her, not accusing her?"

"Okay," Tess said gently. "Let's think about next steps."

"She said the security camera at the bank was out," LuAnn said. "But someone at the bank has to know something. Surely someone saw her or has some record of her being there."

"We can start there," Tess said.

"There were checks in that bank bag too," Janice said. "It's probably worth checking with the people who wrote them to make sure they haven't been cashed or deposited somewhere."

"Cashed?" Tess's eyes widened. "Wouldn't the checks be made out to the Marietta Food Pantry? How could the thief cash a check made out to someone else?"

"Sadly, it's not that difficult," Janice said. "They would just endorse the check and cash it, either at the bank or at a check-cashing place. Banks are supposed to ask for ID, but it probably wouldn't be all that difficult to get around that."

"Or get false paperwork made up with the name of the charity," LuAnn added. "For the amount of money that was in the bag, it would probably be worth it."

"The good news is there would be a paper trail, which might lead us to the thief," Janice said.

Tess sighed. "In that case, let's definitely talk to the people and businesses that wrote checks."

"It sounds like we have a plan," LuAnn said.

Janice still couldn't believe Zelda was in the middle of this. But she would do everything she could to get her out of it.

———

Tess and LuAnn went downstairs to help with lunch, but Janice was antsy. This was Zelda, her son's soon-to-be fiancée, who was in trouble. Janice couldn't just hang around and serve soup when she could be out there finding out what happened to that money. LuAnn and Tess encouraged her to go, so she pulled on her coat and headed to the Sassy Seamstress. Janice had collected a check from Wendy Wilson for the meal, and she would ask Wendy whether the check had been cashed or not.

Janice headed out the side door toward the sewing shop a few blocks away. It was a beautiful late fall day, the air crisp and not a cloud in the deep blue sky. Her nerves settled a little more with each step she took. When she arrived at the shop, she peered through the glass, beyond the artfully draped red and green quilts and framed needlepoint designs of poinsettias and Christmas trees that decorated the holiday-themed window display, and saw that the place was packed. The bells on the door jingled as she stepped inside the former bait shop, now a cozy space filled from floor to rafters with bolts of colorful fabrics, yarns, and patterns along with samples of quilts created by local ladies.

Where once there was a lingering scent of bait, today there was the definite smell of cinnamon and apples in the air. There were twinkling Christmas lights draped along the shelves, and a fabric-themed tree stood in one corner covered with all sorts of sewing and needlework items.

Wendy Wilson, daughter of Grant Grimes and owner of the Sassy Seamstress, hurried over to hug her. With her dark hair caught up in one of those messy buns the younger generation loved to wear, Wendy looked more like a teenager than a successful businesswoman. Today she wore burgundy jeans and a gray T-shirt under a faded denim jacket. On the front of the shirt was an antique sewing machine above a slogan that said: I DON'T HAVE TOO MUCH FABRIC; MY SEWING ROOM IS JUST TOO SMALL.

"I'm so glad you're here, Janice," she exclaimed, her blue eyes sparkling. "We've missed you. Ladies, look who's here!"

Janice looked around and realized that many of her friends were here. There was Jessica Landry, the letter carrier who delivered mail to the inn on weekdays, and Charlotte Bickerton, as well as Brandi Sue, who was the receptionist at Much Kneaded Massage, and Jody, whom Janice had taught with for many years. Janice realized that it was a meeting of the Lunch Bunch Club, a gathering where ladies brought lunch and worked on their projects together. Janice enjoyed the club, but with the busy season at the inn in full swing, she hadn't attended in a few months.

"What did you bring to work on?" Wendy asked.

Janice shook her head. "Actually, I didn't come to work on a project. Although I wish I had. I was actually hoping to talk to you." She looked around the shop, hoping to find a space where they could speak without being overheard. "Maybe we could step back that way?" She pointed to the notions section at the back of the shop.

"Of course. Just one second." Wendy turned to the women gathering at the folding tables and said, "Please go ahead and get started. I'll be with you in just a moment." She led Janice to the rear of the store. "What's going on?"

Janice stood between a rack of zippers and a display of thread. "I wanted to ask you about the check you donated for the Thanksgiving Feast."

"Of course. Is something wrong with it? There was enough in the account, I'm sure of it."

"No, nothing like that." Janice had accidentally bounced a few checks in her life and understood Wendy's fear. It was not only embarrassing; it came with hefty fees. "It's just that, well, I was wondering if you could tell me whether the check you wrote has been deposited or cashed."

At Wendy's confused look, Janice realized she had better explain. "Please try to keep this quiet, but it seems that the donations for the Thanksgiving Feast and food pantry have...Well, they've gone missing. So we were hoping to find out if the checks have been cashed, as that might lead us to whoever is responsible."

"Oh dear." Wendy's concern was evident on her face. "That's terrible. Are people still going to be able to get food delivered or come to the church for their Thanksgiving meal?"

"We sure hope so," Janice said. "That's why we're trying to track down the money."

"Right." Wendy nodded. "That makes sense. Okay, hang on. I'll go check the store's bank account and let you know. Why don't you go visit while I look that up?"

Janice smiled and wandered back toward the front of the store. She said hello to several friends who had just come in and then took a seat next to Jessica Landry. Today Jessica wore jeans and a sweatshirt with a Thanksgiving turkey on it rather than her post office uniform.

"I'm surprised to see you here. Aren't you supposed to be working today?" Janice asked.

Jessica's smile matched her own. "I traded with a coworker on Saturday and took his route. Since that meant I had today off, I decided to do something fun. With that child of mine in school today, Mama is gonna play."

"I can't think of a better place to be," Janice said. "And I love your Thanksgiving sweatshirt." Janice also loved that it was not a Christmas sweatshirt.

"Thank you." Jessica was working on a crocheted blanket in lovely soft shades of pinks and blues.

"And that's beautiful. Is it a baby gift?"

Jessica nodded. "My sister's first is due in March. I'm so excited to be an auntie." She blew out her breath. "Though after the trouble my own child has given me recently, I almost feel like I should be sending a condolence card."

Janice laughed because she knew Jessica was kidding. "I remember those days. My daughter was a challenge more times than I care to remember. Stuart too, though he was more creative in the ways he tried to make me crazy." She shook her head. "So what has Hayley been up to?"

"Oh, you know. The usual. Forgetting her homework. Forgetting her gymnastics outfit. Forgetting to tell me about her Girl Scout meetings. Just generally forgetting things." She laughed. "She's at that age where she thinks she can do things on her own, but she can't."

Janice nodded. She remembered those days.

"Yeah. Well, she 'helped' me at work on Saturday for a Take Your Child to Work Day project for school, and I've got the scars to prove it."

Jessica pulled the sleeve of her sweatshirt up and showed off a bandage taped to her forearm.

"Oh, my. What hap—"

"What is that smell?" Charlotte Bickerton plopped herself down into the chair on the other side of Jessica. "That smells amazing."

Janice and Jessica looked at each other for a moment, and then they both realized Charlotte was referring to the chicken pot pie in front of Jessica.

"This? It's frozen pot pie," Jessica said, shrugging. "Eighty-nine cents at Finn's Family Foods. Pop it in the microwave for five minutes, and you're done."

"Well, it smells delicious." Charlotte sighed and then reluctantly pulled a container of salad and a baggie of carrot sticks from her tote bag.

"Would you like some?" Jessica pushed the pot pie in its cardboard container toward her.

"Oh, no. Thank you, though." Another sigh. "Paul and I are trying to eat better, get more exercise, and adopt a healthier lifestyle."

Janice knew that Charlotte was dating the manager at the bank, Paul Townsend. "Good for you," she said. "That's admirable. And it's nice when couples tackle something like that together."

"Well," she said with a grin, "it's also partly because I want to fit into that wedding dress I've had my eye on, and I want my groom to look as good as I plan to."

"Charlotte," Janice exclaimed. "Are you and Paul—"

"Shh," she interrupted. "Not yet, but soon, I hope. In the meantime, we are both in training for our best lives, so don't say a word."

"Oh, I promise," Jessica said as she appeared to be biting back any further comments. Charlotte pulled her quilting project out of her bag and started chatting with Jody on her other side. Jessica turned to Janice. "She's already as skinny as a twig. What does she need to lose weight for?"

"Well, maybe they only had the dress she likes in a size smaller than she currently wears," Janice offered.

"I suppose," Jessica said with a chuckle. "But she's going to have her hands full keeping that banker out of LotzaBurger, so I hope his tux has an adjustable waistband." She reached for her fork. "Not that I am judging. I like a good burger myself."

"So do I," Janice agreed. "So anyway, what happened to your ar—"

"Janice?"

Janice looked up and saw that Wendy was gesturing for her. She looked back at Jessica apologetically.

"It's okay." Jessica nodded toward her arm. "It looks worse than it is." She smiled and thanked Janice for chatting, and Janice pushed herself up and walked to where Wendy was waiting by the rack of thread.

"I checked online, and the check I wrote hasn't been deposited or cashed," Wendy said. "Should I contact my bank and put a hold on it?"

"That might be a good idea," Janice said. "But it's good news that no one has tried to cash it yet."

"It certainly is." Wendy glanced toward the women. "I should probably get back and make sure these ladies don't go crazy and break out the bedazzler."

Janice laughed and waved goodbye to the ladies and headed out into the bright fall day. She decided to make a couple more stops before heading home, and she went next door to Jasmine Tea Shop, which was another place she'd solicited a donation for the Thanksgiving Feast. Lucy Pearson, the owner, checked the store's bank account online and confirmed that the check she'd written hadn't been cashed or deposited, and Janice suggested she put a stop on the check, which Lucy gratefully promised to do. On the way out of the store, Janice saw a lemon verbena tea in a pretty canister that LuAnn would love and considered buying it for her for Christmas, but she stopped herself. There was plenty of time to go Christmas shopping after Thanksgiving.

She stopped in at Morrison's Books and then at McHappys, and both owners confirmed that the checks they'd written hadn't been deposited or cashed. Janice returned home, simultaneously grateful that the thief hadn't cashed the checks and disappointed that she was returning without learning anything helpful.

After she got back to the inn and helped the others clear up from lunch, they all set out for the bank together. LuAnn drove while Tess and Janice volleyed ideas back and forth.

"Maybe the thief took the cash and just left the checks alone," Tess said. "That way there's far less risk of being caught."

"True, but the bigger donations were checks," Tess said. "So the thief would be missing out on most of the money."

"But wouldn't you rather have part of the money scot-free than risk getting caught?" Janice asked.

"I wouldn't take any of it," Tess pointed out. "So it's hard for me to imagine what a thief might be thinking."

"Fair enough," Janice said.

As LuAnn pulled into the bank's parking lot, Janice studied the building's imposing facade. Built of light-gray stone, it had fluted columns holding up a curved pediment, and the words Marietta Savings Bank were spelled out in bronze letters by the door. It had been built back in an era when bankers tried to instill confidence through stately, solid architecture meant to convince customers that their money was safe within. The people who built this bank could never have imagined a day when you could deposit a check with your phone, Janice thought. The parking lot was at the back of the building, and the ATM and night deposit box were built into the side.

Tess led the way up the marble steps and into the bank's spacious lobby with LuAnn and Janice following a few steps behind. Other than a few customers standing in line at the row of tellers, the lobby was deserted. Tess led the way through the lobby toward the hallway that went to Paul Townsend's office. Janice followed, but movement out of the corner of her eye caught her attention. A teller had turned and was hurrying into the back, her brown ponytail swinging. The customer she'd been helping was craning her neck, trying to see where she'd gone. The teller must have gone to the back to get a form or something, Janice thought. She continued to follow Tess down the hallway.

"May I help you?" someone called from behind them.

Janice turned to see a young lady in a navy skirt and matching blazer with the bank logo on the lapel hurrying after them. Her name badge indicated that her name was Mandy O'Hara.

"We're hoping to have a few minutes of Mr. Townsend's time," Janice told her. "Is he here?"

"Is he expecting you?" Mandy asked.

"No, but I know he'll want to see us," Tess said. "You can tell him it's the crew from Wayfarers Inn."

Mandy didn't seem to know what to do with that, but after a pause, she said, "I think he might be in a meeting. But I'll check."

Tess grinned and set off down the hall again. "No need. We'll just pop in, and if he's busy we'll come back," she tossed over her shoulder as she knocked twice then opened the door to Paul's office.

LuAnn hurried to follow, leaving Janice to offer an apologetic look to Mandy. "I'll let Paul know this interruption is not your fault."

"But—"

Janice left Mandy standing in the hall and walked into the office behind LuAnn. She found Paul Townsend behind a desk piled high with stacks of papers and files. In one hand he held a handful of LotzaBurger fries, and in the other he lifted a can of Sugar Pop soda to his lips.

When his gaze met Janice's, Paul froze. In one swift move, he lowered the can of soda and dumped the fries in the green and yellow LotzaBurger bag and packed it away in his desk drawer.

"We won't tell Charlotte," Tess said as she settled herself on the chair nearest the window. LuAnn and Janice took spots in the next two chairs, leaving the one by the door empty. LuAnn pulled her notebook out of her purse and opened it to the page of notes about the missing money.

"Tell her what?" he said with a grin.

"Right," Tess said.

"Let me guess. You're here to ask about that missing deposit."

"Nailed it in one," Tess said.

Janice looked at Tess. Was that even a phrase? But Paul didn't seem to care.

"Unfortunate all the way around. Just when you think you know someone, that person turns out to be completely different than you expect."

"We're not at all convinced that Zelda was responsible for the money going missing," Janice said firmly.

LuAnn reached over to pat her arm. Though she said nothing, the look that passed between them comforted Janice.

"You're right, of course," Paul said. He must have heard the edge in her voice. "But. Well…I'm not really allowed to say very much about this. But let's just say, this wouldn't be the first red flag as far as her financial history."

"What?" Janice didn't like what he was insinuating. "What are you trying to say?"

"A client's financial records are confidential," he said. "But I can tell you that at one time she applied for a mortgage."

"Okay…" Janice waited for him to go on.

"That's all I can say, I'm afraid."

That was next to nothing. Why even bother to say anything at all if that was all he could tell her?

"The upshot is, we're at an impasse," Paul said. "Miss McLoughlin swears she deposited the money Saturday afternoon. My staff tells me the money was not in the night deposit drawer when it was opened on Monday morning." He shrugged. "Those are the facts, much as I dislike them."

"Who empties the night deposit box on Monday mornings?" Janice asked.

"That day, it was Tara Gordon." After a moment he added, "She's worked here for many years, and I trust her completely."

Out of the corner of her eye, Janice saw LuAnn write the name down in her notebook. They would want to talk to Tara.

"Were you on the property?" LuAnn asked.

"Me?" He paused. "I was here on Monday. Not on Saturday."

LuAnn made a note in her book, then looked up at him again. "Who is usually here on Saturdays?"

He seemed to consider the question for a moment. "We have a few tellers here, but we're only open until noon. And we're not open at all on Sundays."

"So there wouldn't have been anyone on the premises when the deposit was made?" Tess asked.

"No."

LuAnn wrote something else in her notebook.

"Zelda tells us that the security cameras that are focused on the deposit box weren't working the evening the deposit was made," Tess said. "Can you tell us how that happened?"

Paul let out a sigh. "It's awful, isn't it? It makes me crazy. And I really hope that it doesn't get out." He gave them each a significant look. "It would hardly make our depositors feel safe leaving their money with us if it got out that our security had been breached."

"We won't tell," Janice promised. A hundred years ago, it had been stone pillars that made depositors feel safe; these days, it was security cameras.

"The truth is, we've been dealing with a lot of vandalism in the past couple of weeks," Paul said. "It started on Halloween with graffiti. Bad words, lewd images, that sort of thing." He shook his head. "Do you know how hard it is to scrub spray paint off stone?"

"The custodial staff at the school where I worked used to complain about it," LuAnn said, nodding.

"Then it was the firecracker in the night deposit slot right about a week ago. And the broken window on the second floor."

"How did—"

"A baseball," Paul said, shaking his head. "But I think my favorite was when they put a salmon fillet in a deposit envelope and pushed it through the mail slot. By the time we found it Monday morning, the whole place smelled like rotting fish. It took weeks for the smell to clear."

Tess laughed and then looked guilty.

"Who would do such a thing?" LuAnn asked.

Paul shrugged. "We can see from the security camera footage that it's three young guys, but they always wear ski masks, so we haven't been able to identify them."

"And you think these same guys vandalized your security cameras this weekend?"

He nodded. "It happened at some point Friday night. They used baseball bats to smash each of the outdoor security cameras."

Janice couldn't believe it. "Why would someone do all that?"

"At first we assumed it was just kids being dumb. After the third or fourth time, though, we started to wonder."

"Someone with a vendetta against the bank?" Tess asked.

"It started not long after we had to foreclose on a property," he said. "I can't say too much, and I don't know anything for sure, because we haven't been able to get proof. But I would bet they're connected."

"That's really unfortunate," LuAnn said.

"And not just for us," Janice added.

"I know," Paul said. "If we had security footage, we would be able to prove whether Zelda had been here or not. But as it is, there's no way to prove she ever made that deposit. As far as we know, that money never entered this bank."

Janice thought there was a pretty easy way—they should believe her. But she knew it was going to take more than that to get this fixed.

"So there's no recourse?" Tess asked. "No way to prove she deposited the money?"

"I'm bringing in an auditor," Paul said. "To check through all of the deposits that came in over the weekend and see if any of them were somehow assigned to the wrong account. Perhaps that will turn up some answers."

"Let's hope so," Janice said.

There was a light knock, and then Mandy opened the door and stepped in. "I'm sorry, Mr. Townsend, but Miss Bickerton is here. She insists it is urgent."

"Stall her." Paul rose and thrust the trash can toward Mandy. "And get rid of this," he said as he returned to his desk and took a can of air freshener out of a drawer.

A moment later, Paul's office smelled like sandalwood and cinnamon just in time for the door to open again. "Pookie

Bear, it's just me. I have something to show you, and it just cannot..." Charlotte's words stalled when she met Janice's surprised gaze. "Oh, hello, ladies. I didn't realize you were here."

"Obviously," Paul said, his cheeks turning pink.

Charlotte clutched a cookbook with the title *Your First Cleanse.* Poor Paul. He was about to go on a juice diet, and he didn't even know it.

"We were just leaving." Janice turned her attention back to Paul. "If we have any more questions, we'll give you a call. I hope you don't mind."

"Not at all," he told her. "I'll help if I can."

"Thank you." Tess rose, and Janice and LuAnn did the same.

"See you at the meeting Saturday," Charlotte called as they made their way down the hall.

"Really?" Janice turned to face her.

"Yes." She grinned. "I wouldn't miss it for the world."

"See you then," Janice told her.

"I didn't know she was on the committee," LuAnn whispered to Janice once they were on their way to the exit.

Janice shook her head. "She's not."

"Interesting." Tess opened the door, and they stepped out into the afternoon sunshine. "Maybe she's just coming to see what happens. I suspect there'll be a few who will do that."

"I suppose," Janice said. "I just feel awful for how all of this will affect the folks who depend on the feast for their meal that day. What if the bag really is lost, and replacement funds can't be raised?"

"We won't let that happen," LuAnn said.

Janice glanced toward the counter again on the way out, but the teller with the ponytail had been replaced by a man with black hair. It had probably been nothing, she thought. She was just seeing mysteries everywhere, hoping for a clue.

They stepped out of the bank and walked around to the side parking lot, standing just beyond the wall with the ATM and the night deposit box.

"Well, that wasn't very informative," LuAnn said.

"We did learn a few things, though."

Janice appreciated that Tess was trying to be optimistic, but she didn't share the feeling.

"We learned that Paul doesn't believe Zelda ever made the deposit, but he has no way to prove it. So it's just her word against his." LuAnn sighed.

"We also learned that there are some very creative hoodlums in this town," Tess said. "With a strange vendetta against the bank."

Janice knew that Tess was trying to lighten the mood, but she wasn't ready to move past this yet.

"And what was that about Zelda's applying for a mortgage? What does that have to do with anything?" Janice asked.

"Ah. I had a thought about that," LuAnn said. "The house where she lives now, does she own it?"

"No, I don't think so," Janice said. "She's just moved back and wasn't sure how long she would be in town, so she wanted to rent for a while until things were more settled. And it's a good thing too, because presumably she'll move in with Stuart once they're married, so there's no hassle with selling the house."

"Did she tell you that?"

"I...Well...I don't know. Maybe Stuart did. But in any case, what does it..." Her voice trailed off as she saw what LuAnn was hinting at. "You're suggesting she was turned down for a mortgage."

"It sounds like she applied for one," Tess said. "Which doesn't jive with the story you heard, wherever it came from."

"Even if that's true, there are all kinds of reasons why she could have been turned down. A musician's income is hardly steady. Or maybe she didn't have enough saved for a down payment. Home prices have gone up in this area recently," Janice said.

"Or, maybe there was something in her credit history that gave the bank doubts," LuAnn said.

It was possible, Janice realized. But it was hardly proof of anything. "I'll ask Stuart," she said.

There was a moment of quiet, and then LuAnn spoke in the relentlessly cheerful voice that said she was trying to change the subject. "Do you ladies have time to make one more stop before we head home?"

"Sure," Tess said, and Janice agreed.

"How about stopping by the places that Zelda visited before she made the deposits? Maybe someone can verify that they saw the bank bag, or maybe they saw something else relevant."

"Now seems like a good time to do that," Janice said.

"Are you sure you aren't just angling for a reason to go to the Better Batter?" Tess asked.

"Hey. Have a little faith here." A smile spread over LuAnn's face. "I mean, that's not the *whole* reason."

A few minutes later they were walking into the bakery, which was decorated in shades of bright pink and lime green. The glass case along one wall was filled with cupcakes and muffins and breads of every kind.

"Hello!" Sandie Ballard called out as they stepped inside. She'd only opened the bakery a few months back, but it had already become a beloved fixture in town, and Janice knew that Sandie had volunteered to donate dozens of rolls to the Thanksgiving Feast. "Wow. All three of you at once. What a treat."

"Hi, Sandie." LuAnn gave a jaunty wave and looked down at the pastry case. "Oh my. Those chocolate croissants look amazing."

"They are pretty good, if I do say so myself," Sandie said. Sandie had gorgeous blond hair, and Janice could never figure out how she could stay so thin with all the baking she did.

"I'll take one of those," LuAnn said.

"And I'll take a slice of lemon poppy seed cake," Tess said. It was glazed with a thick layer of icing and looked delicious, Janice had to admit.

"And how about you, Janice?" Sandie asked as she put their choices on small white plates.

"My treat," LuAnn said.

"Oh dear." Janice hadn't been planning to have a treat, not this close to dinner, not with Thanksgiving and all the food that came with it just over a week away. But how could she say no now?

"I'll take a pumpkin muffin," she said. That at least had some nutritional value, didn't it?

"Coming right up." Sandie put Janice's muffin on a plate, and as LuAnn counted out the money, Tess asked Sandie if she remembered seeing Zelda and Ellen come in Saturday.

"Oh yeah, Zelda was here. And Ellen—is that the girl who was with her? Sweatshirt? Surly attitude?"

"That's her," Janice said.

"I didn't think she looked like her daughter. Who is she?"

Janice explained that Ellen was staying with Zelda, who was mentoring her, and then asked what time they came in.

"Oh, I don't know, maybe two thirty or so? Zelda got a cupcake, but Ellen didn't get anything."

"I'll never understand some people," Tess said as she took the plate with her slice of cake from the top of the glass case.

"Did you happen to notice Zelda's purse while they were here?" LuAnn asked.

"Her purse?" Sandie shook her head. "I can't say I did. Why?"

"So you didn't see if anything was inside it?" Janice asked.

"No, I didn't." Now Sandie just sounded confused.

"And they didn't leave anything behind?"

"Not that I know of," Sandie said. "Is everything all right?"

"Everything is fine," LuAnn said. "We're just searching for something that we think might have fallen out of Zelda's purse."

Or been taken from it, Janice thought.

"If you tell me what it was, it might be easier for me to be on the lookout," Sandie said.

Tess, LuAnn, and Janice all looked at each other, and then LuAnn shrugged and explained.

Sandie's mouth formed an *O*, and she shook her head. "*All* the money for the Thanksgiving Feast?"

"I'm afraid so," Janice said. "And for the food pantry drive."

"Oh dear. No, I definitely didn't see anything like that around here, but if I find it, I'll be sure to let you know."

They all thanked her and then they finished their treats before they climbed back into LuAnn's car and drove the few blocks to Olive, the trendy clothing store on the corner of Fifth Street. Large plate-glass windows faced the street on the ground level, and the upper two floors of the brick building had shutters at the windows. Inside, loud music played through hidden speakers, and the floors and walls were filled with displays of T-shirts, sneakers, and accessories.

"Hi there." An impossibly thin young woman in skinny jeans and a chunky knit sweater came toward them. "Welcome to Olive. Can I help you find something?"

If she was surprised to see three middle-aged women enter the store, she didn't show it, though Janice was certain no one their ages had ever bought this clothing for themselves. She could see how Ellen would like it though. She was the right age for this stuff.

"We're actually hoping you can help us with something," Tess said. "Our friend was in here Saturday afternoon, and we're wondering if she may have left something behind."

"What was it?" the woman asked. "I was here all day Saturday."

"It was a bank bag," Tess said.

The woman stared at them. Janice glanced at the price tag on a T-shirt with a picture of a banana on it. *Fifty dollars?* Fifty dollars for a T-shirt with a banana on it? Janice did not understand the world sometimes.

"It's a small rectangle, about this big." Luann held out her hands about the size of a shoe box. "Black, with a zipper along one side."

"Oh. Like a cosmetics case."

"Sure," Tess said. "Have you seen anything like that?"

"I'm afraid not."

They then asked if she remembered seeing Ellen and Zelda, and while she did remember women matching that description, she hadn't noticed what either of them had in their purses. They thanked her and asked her to let them know if she remembered anything about the encounter. She promised to do so, and they all piled into LuAnn's car and headed back to the inn.

"I don't know if any of that helped," LuAnn said as they drove through the cobbled streets of the historic town.

"I'm sure it did," Tess said. "I'm just not sure how yet."

Janice hoped she was right. Because she pretty much agreed with LuAnn on this one.

Chapter Six

November 2, 1859

Prudence settled the sleeping child, a little girl, next to Moses in the crib. Made by Jason for their little girl who did not live long enough to sleep in it, the little bed was now full. And, for a moment, so was Prudence's heart.

Silence filled the room, broken only by the swish of the trees outside the window as the wind tossed their limbs. Moses shifted in his sleep, but the infant seemed not to notice.

Moving to the edge of the bed, Prudence watched the pair as they slumbered. Then the front door closed.

Jason was home.

Prudence gave a moment's thought to hiding the child from him until she absolutely had to reveal she was here, but good sense quickly prevailed. Tiptoeing from the bedroom, she greeted her husband with a kiss.

"Something is amiss."

A statement, not a question. How did he always know?

Prudence reached out to grasp Jason's hand. "We have a guest," she whispered.

Confusion clouded his handsome features. "Why are you speaking so softly?"

"Come and see."

She led him to the bedroom and then released her grip. Nodding to the cradle, she paused at the door. After a moment, Jason walked over to where his son was sleeping.

He looked up, and their eyes met. Then he walked away, pressing past her to retrace his steps to the front door.

Prudence found him sitting on the porch steps, his arms resting on his knees and his head lowered. Though her footsteps caused the porch to creak, Jason gave no notice that he knew she had followed him.

Even when she settled on the step beside him, he remained still and quiet, his eyes focused on the ground. She sat very still, adding her own prayers to whatever conversation it appeared Jason was having with the Lord.

"Where did the child come from?" he finally asked.

"I found her, down by the path."

"Is she a package?"

"I do not know," she confessed. "I had no warning of one. But there was no sign of anyone who cared for her. I could not just leave her."

"No," Jason said. "Of course thee could not."

"She would not have survived if I had left her."

"I know." Jason took a deep breath. "A baby will not be easy to hide."

"Perhaps we don't have to hide her." As the words came out, Prudence realized she had already let herself hope that the child could become theirs. That they could care for this abandoned babe.

"For now, she must remain a secret," Jason said. "If anyone were to find her, and she is not free…" He let his voice trail off. "It could ruin everything,"

Prudence nodded, knowing he was right. By bringing this baby into their home, she may have just put them all in very grave danger.

CHAPTER SEVEN

Janice was reading the lead story in the *Marietta Times* Wednesday morning when Stuart came to pick up the ring. The headline read TENS OF THOUSANDS OF DOLLARS LOST; TOWN THANKSGIVING FEAST IN PERIL.

"Don't read that. It will just make you angry," Stuart said.

"It's a bit over the top," Janice agreed. "Tens of thousands of dollars?"

Stuart shrugged. "That might not be too far off. The people of this town are generous. But it also insinuates that Zelda was responsible for the money's disappearance, which doesn't do her career any favors."

Janice closed the paper. She had other questions to ask Stuart, but the café was full of guests, so Janice ushered him into the kitchen, out of earshot, to ask him about the missing money. Winnie was working at Big Red, frying pancakes. She might be able to hear, but Janice decided that was all right.

"Has she looked for the bag at home or in her car?" Janice asked.

"She's looked everywhere," he said. "And so have I. We've turned her house and car upside down. We even traced her steps over the weekend and looked at the recording studio—

where she went on Sunday, well after she deposited the money—and the pizza place where she got the pizza after she deposited the money. She confirmed with the manager that nothing was left behind."

"Stuart, please don't take this the wrong way," Janice said, "but did you search Ellen's room carefully?"

The pause in their conversation gave Janice cause to regret the question.

"Yes," he finally said. "And I hate to say it, but Ellen was the first person I thought of when I heard what was going on. I don't know how much you know about her."

"Just what Zelda said on Saturday. That she's had a rough life, and Zelda has hopes of showing her a better way to live."

"She thinks she can, but I've had my doubts from the beginning. Now Zelda is beginning to wonder too."

"Does Zelda have reason to believe Ellen stole the money?"

"If she does, she hasn't said specifically. All I know is when Zelda and I announced to Ellen and Brin that we needed to do a thorough search of their rooms, not because we believed they were guilty but just to eliminate the possibility that something accidentally caused it to end up in one of their rooms, neither girl seemed pleased."

"Brin too?" she said.

"Yes." He sighed. "I didn't say anything to Zelda, but while she was looking through Ellen's room, I could have sworn I saw Brin trying to hide something, maybe an envelope, in the pocket of her hoodie."

"But not the bank bag?"

"No, it was too small for that. Brin was just acting odd, which isn't like her. That made me suspicious."

"Did you ask her about it?" Janice said.

"What could I say?" Stuart paused. "I did mention it to Zelda, but she laughed it off. Said maybe she made a bad grade on a test and didn't want her to see it. Apparently Brin spends so much time at school that she isn't capable of doing anything but eating and sleeping at home anymore and has no other interests except her studies. At least that was her mother's answer."

"And you accepted that answer?"

He paused again. "I have for now, but I love Zelda, and I'll do whatever I have to do to prove she didn't steal those donations. If it means questioning Brin again, then I will. And Ellen too. I've even thought about ways to try to come up with the money to cover the missing donations, but aside from selling my house or my car, I don't see how I could."

"Oh, Stuart, you can't do that," Janice said.

"Even if I wanted to, Zelda has said she would never allow it."

"Of course she wouldn't," Janice said. "She wouldn't want you to take that risk for her."

"She's fiercely independent, which is what I love about her, but not when it comes to something as serious as this. She said she'd have to pay me back, and she couldn't promise she'd be able to. Of course I told her I wouldn't want her to pay me back, but..." He sighed.

Janice remembered her conversation at the bank the day before. "Stuart, has anything like this ever happened to Zelda before?"

"Like what?"

"Like..." How did she phrase this carefully? "Like, is she good with money?"

"I believe so," he said. "Why?"

"It's just..." Janice took a deep breath. "When we were at the bank yesterday, Paul Townsend said something about Zelda applying for a mortgage and suggested she'd been turned down."

"She's never mentioned it to me," Stuart said.

"So she didn't apply for a mortgage?" Janice asked.

"She started out thinking she might. But in the end she decided she wasn't ready for a commitment like home ownership. But I'll ask her about it."

"If you're going to get married, it's important to know," Janice said. And then, when he didn't answer right away, she continued, "You are still planning to propose, right?"

"I don't know, Ma," he said. "Zelda is focused on this problem right now, which is as it should be, but I'm struggling whether to propose now and give her something positive to focus on or to wait until the deposit is found and then pop the question."

"I think you need to wait until this situation is resolved," she said. "That's about as helpful as I can be. I know I asked you to hurry, but that was me being selfish. I'm just terrible at keeping secrets." Her heart sank. "Just be sure you do a lot of praying about it."

"I will, Ma," he said. He picked up the velvet pouch with the ring inside, tucked it into his briefcase, and gave Janice a hug before he headed out to work.

Janice leaned back against the counter, trying to muster the energy to put a smile on her face before she went out to help serve breakfast.

"Want to talk about it?" Winnie finally said.

Janice nodded. "I guess you overheard all that."

"I did."

Janice let out a long breath. "The bank is going to call in an auditor to see if something went wrong with the deposit and the money went into the wrong account. I keep hoping that's what happened here."

"Yes, Lord, please let that be the case," Winnie said. "But what if it isn't?"

"If it isn't, then we need to figure out what happened to it. And quickly, because the Thanksgiving Feast is only eight days away, and if there's no money to pay for it..."

"Then there will be plenty of people who don't get to have a Thanksgiving meal this year." Winnie sank down onto the stool across from Janice. "All right then. Our job here is clear."

Janice shook her head. "It is?"

"Yes, it is." Winnie reached out to grasp Janice's hands in hers. "First we pray that money is found inside that bank or, if it is outside the bank, it shows up before it's too late. And then we pray that if neither of those things happens, it becomes clear that the Lord has other plans."

Tears filled Janice's eyes, but she didn't want to break the bond between her and Winnie to wipe them away.

"That money will be found," Winnie said. "Just you watch. And here's how I know: that money isn't missing at all. The Lord knows where it is, and He will reveal that at exactly the right time."

CHAPTER EIGHT

After praying with Winnie, Janice called Zelda and asked if they could talk to her about making the deposit on Saturday. Zelda told Janice that she would be recording in the studio that morning and that Ellen was supposed to meet her there to work on a duet at ten, so all three of them piled into Janice's car and headed toward the studio.

"Here goes nothing," Tess said. "Hopefully we'll get some answers today."

They passed warehouses and commercial buildings, as well as a few strip malls that had seen better days. Finally, they found the address Zelda had given them. The recording studio was situated in a nondescript tan building a few miles outside of Marietta. With Tiny Tom's Dry Cleaners on one side and Miracle Mike's Used Office Furniture on the other, there was nothing to distinguish the space as anything special.

A beat-up metal desk that looked as if it had been purchased next door at Mike's held court on one side of a small reception area. Neon lights overhead cast a harsh glow over chipped linoleum floors and an artificial palm tree that somehow looked as if it needed a good watering. The only artwork in the space was a framed poster advertising a concert at the Adelphia Music Hall in Marietta from several years ago.

A gray-haired man appeared in the doorway. He wore a navy argyle cardigan and matching trousers paired with sneakers and a wide smile. He looked more like Mr. Rogers than an employee of a recording studio.

"Welcome. You must be Zelda's friends," he said with the slightest trace of a British accent.

"Yes," Janice said. "We are. I'm Janice, and this is LuAnn and Tess."

"Clive Clinton. I'm Zelda's manager." He nodded toward the hallway. "Come this way. She's expecting you, but she's recording right now."

"How exciting," LuAnn said. "I've never been in a recording studio before."

Clive paused to point to a red line that had been painted on the floor in the hallway between the foyer and the back of the studio. "The only rule of crossing the red line is that when you do, you must remain silent when the musician is recording. Our sound people want to hear only what will be on the record."

"We understand," Tess said as LuAnn and Janice nodded in agreement.

"Excellent," he said. "Then follow me."

They continued down the hallway a few steps and then turned to the right and entered a massive studio space. The walls were covered in sound-proofing that looked like egg crates, and a sheet of glass separated them from the space where Zelda would be singing. To their left, two young men with beards and ponytails leaned over a soundboard that was ten times larger than the one at church.

Neither of them paid any attention as the ladies were ushered to stools that had been arranged in one corner. Other people bustled around, but Janice was focused on her future daughter-in-law.

On the other side of the glass, Zelda stood in front of a microphone with her eyes closed. The older man gave the signal to the fellows at the sound booth, and the first chords of music swelled.

Janice's singing experience was limited to the church choir and the trio she, LuAnn, and Tess had formed in college. Hearing Zelda sing praise and worship music in the studio, however, was awe inspiring. When she closed her eyes, it felt as if this just might be what the soundtrack of heaven sounded like.

From their spot they could watch the process of recording a song while remaining out of the way of the many people it took to complete the task. From the person at the soundboard to the musicians and various other studio personnel, the place buzzed with activity. But on the other side of the glass, Zelda sang as if she was alone with the Lord, oblivious to anyone else.

Too soon, the singing ended. Zelda took off her headphones and stepped away from the microphone to wave at Janice.

"All right," the man at the sound booth said over the speaker. "We'll break for ten minutes."

Zelda disappeared through a door in the back of the sound booth and arrived at Janice's side. "You sounded amazing," Janice gushed. "Just amazing." LuAnn and Janice nodded in agreement.

Zelda smiled. "Thank you. I'm grateful I get to do this." Her smile quickly faltered. "I hope I can continue."

"Why wouldn't you? Once we find that bank bag," Janice quickly amended.

"Do you think you will?" Zelda asked, her voice now wavering.

"I do," Janice said firmly. "It's out there somewhere, and I believe we'll find it."

"And we're thankful you were able to set up some time for us to be able to talk to Ellen," LuAnn said.

"Although we're sure she had nothing to do with it," Janice said quickly. "But it will allow us to rule her out."

"That's okay," Zelda said. "I understand. I really hope she had nothing to do with this. But it can't hurt for you to talk to her. Just fair warning, I'm not sure she'll totally agree."

"What makes you say that?"

"Honestly, I think she feels a bit betrayed that Stuart and I searched her room."

"Searching her room seems like a perfectly natural thing to do under the circumstances," Tess said.

"She didn't think so," Zelda said. "My heart just broke when I saw her expression. Stuart and I tried to explain that we weren't accusing her of anything. We just wanted to eliminate any possibility that I had forgotten to drop off the bag and it had somehow ended up in her room."

Janice sighed. "I suppose, given her background, she might not believe you didn't think badly of her." At Zelda's surprised expression, she said, "Stuart filled me in, but only to let me know why she was here with you over the holidays. I didn't mean to sound like I was passing judgment on her, because I certainly am not."

"No, of course not, Janice. You're the kindest woman I know. The truth is, I wondered later if she had something to hide. If she took the bag, she's hidden it well. There was nothing in her room that gave any indication she took the money."

Zelda looked up at the clock on the wall. "And let's hope she gets here soon. We're supposed to start recording that duet in a few minutes, and I can't afford to burn studio time."

"You have to pay for time even when you're not recording?" Tess asked.

"Yes. You pay for the studio by the hour ahead of time, so if she's late, it's just wasting money."

"That hardly seems fair," LuAnn said.

Zelda shrugged. "I have to pay for these guys to be here, whether they're working or not. And thankfully, I don't have to pay them cash today or anything. My record label paid for all of it in advance, and they take it out of any royalties that come in when the album is released."

"Well, that's helpful," Janice said. She looked at LuAnn and Tess. *See,* she wanted to say. *Zelda wouldn't have taken that money, because her label paid for all this.* But Janice knew that argument didn't really hold water. Zelda had made it clear that there were plenty of other expenses she had to cover. A large chunk of cash would still be useful to her.

"I'll just text Brin to make sure they're on their way," Zelda said.

"Brin's coming too?" LuAnn asked.

"She's dropping Ellen off before class. Ellen's car won't start again. It always seems to be broken down."

"That's too bad," Tess said.

"But nice of Brin," Janice said.

"I offered her gas money, but she wouldn't take it," Zelda said. She pulled her phone out of her pocket and tapped the screen.

This could work out well, Janice thought. They'd been hoping to talk to Brin. Maybe they could catch her when she dropped Ellen off.

"They'll be here in a minute," Zelda said. "Thank goodness."

Clive appeared and called Zelda over, and Janice and the others moved to stand in the lobby so they could see out the glass door. A moment later, a ratty blue Jeep that had seen better days turned in to the parking lot and stopped a few spaces down from where the ladies were parked. There was a flower decal on the back window.

"That must be them," LuAnn said. "Since Zelda seems to be in a hurry to get the recording started, what do you say we try to talk to Brin first?"

"That sounds like a plan to me," Tess said.

LuAnn pushed the studio door open just as Ellen climbed out of the car.

"Just one of us should go out and try to catch Brin," Janice said. "Otherwise, it will seem like an ambush."

"You're right," LuAnn said. "Janice, why don't you do it, since you're practically related to her. We'll wait in here."

Ellen's eyes widened when she saw Janice step out the door.

"Hi, Ellen!" Janice tried to make her voice sound natural, but it came out sounding high and squeaky. "Zelda is waiting for you inside."

Ellen's face relaxed when she realized Janice wasn't coming out to talk to her, and she hurried into the studio.

"Brin?" Janice ducked down by the driver's side of the car. "Do you have a second?"

"Hi." Brin's eyes were wide, but she rolled down the window. Janice and Brin had met many times, but hadn't spent much time together on their own lately, and she was no doubt wondering why Janice was approaching her now. "What's going on?"

"I was hoping I could ask you a few questions." Janice felt ridiculous bending over to talk to her through the open window, but Brin made no move to get out of the car. At least the higher body of the Jeep meant she didn't have to crouch. "My friends and I are helping your mom track down the money that's gone missing, and I was hoping you could tell us if you remember seeing it at all. We're trying to verify that she brought it home with her before she got to the bank." Zelda had been sure she'd had the money in her purse when she went home, but it didn't hurt to check. And it was a better way to approach the conversation than demanding to know where Brin had been when the money disappeared.

"Ah, the money." Brin shook her head. "I feel so bad for my mom. She's been so torn up about the whole thing. She feels totally responsible. I don't know what's going to happen if that money doesn't turn up. She's talking about paying it all back herself, and she doesn't have that kind of money."

"That's noble of her," Janice said.

"But unrealistic," Brin said. "Anyway, I'm afraid I can't be much help. I was at the library studying all Saturday afternoon. I stopped in at the house before going to my study group that evening, but didn't talk to Mom. She was on the phone with her manager, and we just waved at each other. I certainly didn't look in her purse. I don't know if the money was there or not." After a pause, she added, "I hope you guys find it. It would mean so much to my mom."

"I heard your mom did a search through the whole house," Janice said.

"Oh, yeah. Ellen was so mad, and all like, 'why don't you trust me,' and moping around. I don't know. She's a year older than I am, but sometimes she seems so young, you know? They looked in my room too, but of course they didn't find anything. But better to check, right?" She lifted one shoulder.

Janice couldn't think of anything else to ask, so after an awkward moment, she said, "Thanks for your help."

"Anytime," Brin said. "I'd better get over to the college. I have a class starting in twenty minutes."

"Of course," Janice said, and straightened up. Brin rolled up the window, and Janice hurried back inside the studio.

"How did it go?" Tess asked.

"All right," Janice said. "She had to run off to class, but she said that she was home briefly on Saturday while her mom was on the phone with Clive. She didn't look inside her mom's purse, so she has no idea if the money was there or not. She mostly seemed concerned with how her mom was doing through all this."

"It does seem unlikely that she would take the money," LuAnn said. "Sure, college is expensive, but she had to know her mom would be the one who got blamed, so why would she do that?"

Janice nodded. "I think we can scratch her off the suspect list."

"I think you're probably right," LuAnn said. She pulled the notebook out of her purse. "But we'll catch Ellen when they're done recording and see what she has to say."

LuAnn glanced down at her watch. "I'll call the inn and let them know we won't be back in time to serve lunch today. It's a good thing both Taylor and Robin are scheduled to work."

They went back into the studio area and watched through the glass as Zelda and Ellen sang a beautiful duet about trusting the Lord even when things look bad. Janice couldn't have thought of a more appropriate message for Zelda right now. She reminded herself again that God knew where that money was even if they didn't.

When they finished recording, Zelda and Ellen came out of the studio.

"Ellen, you've met Tess and Janice before, and this is LuAnn. Ladies, Ellen."

"Hey." Ellen ducked her head, and her bangs swept in front of her eyes. She was wearing another hooded sweatshirt and baggy jeans and white Chuck Taylors with homemade ink drawings all over them.

"These ladies are helping me figure out what happened to the money that disappeared Saturday," Zelda said. She held a plastic water bottle in her hands, and she kept unscrewing the top and screwing it back on. "And since you were with me when I lost it, they wanted to ask for your take on it to make sure I'm not leaving out any details."

She did a good job of making it seem totally innocuous, just a friendly little chat. But Ellen saw right through it, naturally.

"Fine," she said. "Let's get this over with."

Zelda seemed embarrassed by Ellen's hostility. "There's a conference room in the back, if you want to find somewhere with a bit more privacy. And then after that, what do you say we go get some ice cream?"

Zelda was trying just a bit too hard to be upbeat and nonchalant, and Ellen wasn't buying it. "I think I'd rather just go home," she said.

Zelda's smile faded, and Janice's heart broke for her. She was trying to do her best by this girl, Janice could see that, but Ellen wasn't making it easy for her.

"All right. The conference room is back this way. It's not much, and last time I saw it, it was a mess, but it's somewhere you all can talk." Zelda led the way down the hallway and flipped on the light in a small room with scuffed gray walls. There was a table in the middle surrounded by mismatched office chairs, and there were cardboard boxes piled up along the walls holding brochures and T-shirts and who knew what else. "I'll be out front talking to Clive," she said, and then, after one more wide smile, she disappeared down the hallway.

"So," Ellen said, sitting in one of the chairs. "Do you guys think I took the money too?"

"No," LuAnn said. "We don't think that at all. We're just trying to figure out what happened to it and want any details you can provide."

"Uh-huh. Sure." Ellen nodded. "Let's go with that."

Oh dear. This wasn't going well. And, to be honest, Ellen wasn't wrong. They couldn't even fault her for thinking she was a suspect, because she was.

"Your voice is beautiful," Tess said. "That song you just sang with Zelda gave me chills."

"Thanks." Ellen's face relaxed just a tiny bit. "I wrote that song."

"You did?" Janice hoped she didn't sound as surprised as she felt. "It was gorgeous."

"Thank you." Ellen brushed her bangs out of her face, but they fell back in her eyes. "It's what I want to do."

"You're good at it," Janice said, and she meant it. Ellen's voice was stunning, deep, and rich. Suddenly Janice understood why Zelda's manager was willing to take Ellen on and groom her, even when she wasn't making it easy.

"Thanks." She blew out a breath. "Okay. So. You were asking me about the money?"

"You were there at the meeting on Saturday," Janice said. "And saw how much money Zelda collected. Did you see what she did with it afterward?"

"I have to confess I wasn't really paying all that much attention to it," Ellen said. "I figured it was her deal to worry about."

"So you don't know if it was in her purse or not when you left the meeting at the church on Saturday?"

"I really don't know." She toyed with the rubber on the edge of her shoe. "I would assume so, but I didn't check."

"Where did you go after you left the meeting?" They had already heard the list of stops from Zelda, but she wanted to hear the list from Ellen.

"First we stopped at that bakery that's all pink and green everywhere?"

"The Better Batter," Tess said. "I love that place."

"Yeah. Zelda got a cupcake, but I didn't get anything. I seriously don't know how she manages to eat the way she does and stay so thin. I'd literally weigh a thousand pounds."

"And after that?"

"I wanted to go to that cool store over on Fifth and Second. We're doing a concert soon, and I wanted to find something to wear. So we stopped there."

"Did you find anything?"

"They had some cool shirts and this leather jacket I liked. But I didn't buy anything. That store's pretty expensive, and I don't have the money yet." She rolled her eyes. "Okay, I get it. You guys think that's why I stole the money, right? That's my motive?"

None of them said anything. Again, she'd gotten it pretty much right.

"I didn't steal the money," she said.

"Of course you didn't," Tess said in her most soothing voice. "No one said you did. We just want to know if you happened to see the bank bag in Zelda's purse while you were there."

"Sorry. Like I said, I really wasn't paying attention. I assume it was still in her purse, but I don't know." And then, a moment later, she added, "I wasn't planning to steal it, so it didn't seem relevant to know where it was." She gave them a pointed look.

"After you left Olive, you went home, right?" LuAnn asked, ignoring the attitude.

"Yes," Ellen said. "I went to my room. And by the way, I did not take the money with me. Zelda made some phone calls."

Tess started to open her mouth, and Ellen held up her hand. "And before you ask what I was doing, I was working on a new song. I wasn't hiding cash in a mattress or anything crazy like that."

"I'm glad to hear it," Tess said. "And then what happened?"

"And then she made me come with her to deposit the money."

"Why did she have you go with her?"

"So I could 'help' choose the kind of pizza for dinner." She used her fingers to make air quotes. "But really it's because Clive asked her to babysit me, to make sure I don't get into trouble, and she's taking that very seriously. So she makes me go everywhere with her." She cast a glance at Janice. "Except on dates with

Stuart. That would be weird. But then she gets Brin to stay with me. It's crazy. I'm older than Brin, you know? I don't need someone to hold my hand all the time."

"That's got to be frustrating," LuAnn said gently.

"Yeah. I mean, if you don't trust me, why let me live in your house at all?"

"Do you know why she agreed to it?" LuAnn asked.

"Because Clive made her."

"Because she wants to help," Janice said.

"Yeah, well, she has a strange way of showing it. Accusing me of stealing the money for poor people's Thanksgivings. What does she think I am?"

"I'm sure she didn't mean to accuse you," Janice said. "She's just trying to cover all the bases and make sure you couldn't be blamed by someone else."

"Right." Ellen pressed her lips together and nodded. "No doubt."

Janice didn't know what to say, and a moment later, Ellen broke the silence. "Can I go now?"

Another awkward silence, and then LuAnn said, "Thanks for talking to us."

Ellen rolled her eyes and stood. She grabbed her bag, and a moment later she was gone. She left an uncomfortable silence in her wake.

"She seemed really sensitive," Janice finally said.

"Well, sure." Tess leaned back, and her chair creaked. "You probably would be too if you were a guest in someone's home, and they accused you of stealing thousands of dollars."

Janice saw her point, but it was more than that. It somehow felt deeper than that. It was like they had touched a nerve somehow. "Do you think there's any chance she took the money?"

"It's hard to say," LuAnn said. "She's one of the few people with the opportunity. She was with the money almost the whole time."

"And she does have motive," Janice said. "In addition to the expenses of starting a recording career, she apparently needs to have some work done on her car."

"Yeah, but everyone has a motive in this case. I can't think of a single person who doesn't wish they had more money," Tess said. "That's not enough to convince me that she did it."

Janice didn't know what to think.

They gathered their things and went out to the lobby to thank Zelda and Ellen, and then they headed to the car.

By this time, it was well past lunchtime, and Janice's stomach was grumbling.

"Is anyone else starving?" Tess asked as they walked back to the car.

"I am," LuAnn said. "And I haven't stopped thinking about that burger and fries Paul was eating yesterday. It looked so good."

"Why don't we go have lunch there?" Tess asked.

Janice's stomach grumbled, but still she hesitated. "We should probably head back to the inn to help with lunch, shouldn't we?"

"Taylor and Robin have it under control," LuAnn said. "What's the point of owning your own business if you can't blow off work and go out for a burger once in a while?"

Janice tried to find a reason to disagree, but she couldn't.

"Besides, I was thinking about LotzaBurger all last night," Tess said as she buckled herself in to the passenger seat.

"So was I." LuAnn laughed from the back seat.

"Not because it's delicious, although it is," Tess said. "I was thinking about *where* it is."

"Where it is?" Janice pictured the burger joint in her mind. It was downtown, on Putnam Street, in an old brick building that had housed various restaurants on the ground floor over the years, though LotzaBurger seemed to have staying power. The food was so delicious, it was not hard to see why.

"Oh..." LuAnn smacked her forehead. "I can't believe I didn't think of that myself."

Janice still didn't see it. "What do you mean?"

"LotzaBurger is right across the street from the bank," LuAnn said. "Which probably doesn't help poor Paul Townsend on his diet."

"There's nothing to say that they have security cameras," Tess said. "But they might. And it can't hurt to ask, right?"

"Oh!" Janice saw it now. "You're hoping their security cameras might have picked up Zelda making the deposit."

"And anything else that happened after that," Tess said. "I say we go scarf down some burgers and fries while we ask questions." She grinned. "After all, we're only doing our civic duty, right?"

A few minutes later they pulled into the small parking lot behind the burger restaurant and walked inside. The smell of french fries hit them as soon as they walked in. Janice's stomach grumbled again.

"I see a camera under that eave," Tess said, looking out the plate-glass front window. "It's pointed toward the parking lot, but I wonder..."

"Let's ask about it once we're seated," LuAnn said.

They walked toward the hostess stand. "Table for three?" The hostess, a perky young girl in a frilled peach apron, held up three menus.

"Yes, please," LuAnn said, and they followed her back through the restaurant. From the black-and-white checked floor to the red vinyl booths, the place felt like stepping back into an old-fashioned hamburger place in the 1950s. Frank Sinatra crooned an oldie as they settled into an oversized corner booth by the front window.

"I forgot how much I love this place," Tess said. "I'm going to have to bring the grandbabies here. They would love it."

"I thought their mama had 'healthy food only' rules," LuAnn said.

"Well, that's her rule at home." Tess shrugged. "But anything goes when they're with Mimi."

"You don't mean that," Janice said with a grin.

"Just watch me," she responded. "I say we get all the little ones together here soon. Doesn't that sound like fun?"

"The more important question is, what are we having?" Janice asked.

"I'm getting a burger and fries," LuAnn said without even opening her menu. "Make it a cheeseburger, actually. And a milkshake."

"That sounds delicious," Janice said. "But I'll skip the milkshake."

"I'll skip the burger and just get fries and the milkshake," Tess said with a guilty smile.

The waitress arrived with three waters and took their orders, and then she hurried off toward the kitchen.

"Should we just ask for the manager?" LuAnn asked.

"Hang on. I think I may have a connection," Janice said. Last time she'd been in here she'd run into a former student who'd said he was the assistant manager. "I'll go ask."

She climbed out of the booth and headed toward the back. The sounds of metal clanging against metal and the hiss of sizzling oil got louder as she neared the kitchen.

"Can I help you?" The waitress came out of the kitchen carrying two chocolate milkshakes.

"I was wondering if Edwin Reed still works here."

"Oh, sure. Hang on. Let me deliver these before they melt, and I'll see if I can grab him."

She delivered Tess's and LuAnn's milkshakes, and then she passed by Janice again and headed into an office at the back. A minute later, a young man in a button-down shirt and pressed slacks came out. He had only been out of high school a few years, but he looked so grown up.

"Mrs. Eastman." Edwin seemed pleased to see her. He had been a disaster in Home Ec, and Janice was pretty sure he only took it, as many football players did, because he thought it would be an easy way to boost his GPA. But he had been a nice kid, and she'd appreciated his sense of humor, if not his sautéing skills. "It's nice to see you."

"It's good to see you too. I was hoping you still worked here."

"I got a promotion. I'm the manager now." The pride on his face at the title was clear.

"That's really great," Janice said. "I'm glad to hear it."

"What can I do for you?"

"I have a question."

"Well, considering how many of my questions you answered back in high school, answering one of yours is the least I can do," he said with a chuckle. "Ask away."

She asked him about the cameras, and a few minutes later she walked back to the booth and slid into her spot with a broad grin.

"Good news?" Tess asked.

Janice nodded. "See that camera over the front door? They have another one just like it aimed at the side of the bank where the night deposit box is." She paused. "And a third one on the far side of the building that's focused on the front parking lot."

"And their cameras are working?" Tess asked.

"We'll soon find out," she said. "One of my former students is the manager here. I told him what we're investigating, and he agreed to give us a copy of the footage from last weekend."

"That's great news," LuAnn said.

"Yes, it is," Janice agreed. "This could be exactly the proof we need to show that Zelda made that deposit."

"Let's hope it does," Tess said, just as the waitress set three steaming baskets of fries and two cheeseburgers down on the table. "For now, let's eat."

They chatted about their plans for Thanksgiving, and LuAnn told them about one of the guests she'd had a conversation with this morning. It didn't take long before their plates were empty.

Just as they finished paying the bill, Edwin came by with the security camera footage on a thumb drive. "This should show you Saturday and Sunday," he said, handing the drive to Janice. "Let me know if you need anything else."

"Thank you," Janice said, slipping it into her purse. "I really appreciate this."

They made their way to the door quickly. Janice couldn't wait to get home and review the footage. It would only be a matter of time before they could prove that Zelda really did make that donation after all.

But as they stepped out the door, Tess froze. Janice almost bumped into her but stopped herself at the last moment.

"Do you guys see that?" Tess asked.

"See what?" Janice managed to squeeze out from behind Tess and look where she was pointing. "It's the bank."

"Yes, but look in the parking lot." Tess was still pointing, but Janice couldn't see at what.

"Oh, my." LuAnn's mouth fell open. "That can't be her. Right?"

Finally, Janice saw what they were looking at.

"Oh dear." She blinked a couple of times, just to make sure she was seeing it right. "No, it can't be her car. It's got to be another one."

Tess looked at LuAnn, who was already heading toward the street. She followed just a step behind. "There's only one way to find out."

CHAPTER NINE

November 2, 1859

"We can hide the child for a short while," Jason said. "But we must try to find her parents."

Prudence nodded, even though she did not know what kind of parents would leave a babe alone by the river. Parents who did not deserve to care for a child, she thought.

"Thee must be quiet about it, though. If the wrong people were to find out…"

Prudence understood his thinking. She knew their deliveries posed a great risk. But this was different. This was but a babe.

"Prudence," Jason said. "We have a package coming soon…"

He didn't need to go on. She understood his thinking. If people started to ask questions about the child, it could draw attention to their other…visitors.

"I will ask around," Prudence promised. "Someone here will know where the child came from."

"No," Jason said. "I will go and ask around town. You stay here with the babies."

"It is Thursday," Prudence said. "That means we have a few days before our package comes."

"Yes," said Jason. "But a few days is all."

He rose then leaned over and kissed the top of Prudence's head. "Do not wait dinner," he told her. "I may be late."

"Where is thee headed?"

His expression showed weariness and something else. Something she could not quite determine. "To look for a remedy to this."

The door closed softly behind him, and his boots sounded against the steps. She stood and watched through the window. Jason was a good man but a stubborn one. Wherever he was going, he would not quit until he found a solution.

CHAPTER TEN

Janice studied the blue Jeep in the bank parking lot. "It can't be the same one," she said. "Brin told me she was headed to class."

"And yet here she is, at the bank," LuAnn said. "Why is that?"

"There are tons of Jeeps in the world," Janice said. "This isn't hers."

"This one has a flower decal on it, just like hers did," LuAnn said. Janice turned and narrowed her eyes, but LuAnn shrugged. "The whole time you were talking with her, we were staring at the back of the car."

"It's got to be hers," Tess said.

"But why would she tell me she was going to class if she was coming here?" Janice asked.

"That's the million-dollar question," LuAnn said.

"Or at least the several-thousand-dollar question," Tess said.

"Okay." Janice could see she was losing this battle. Those french fries were starting to sour in her stomach. "So what do we do now?"

"We go into the bank and ask her why she lied to you," LuAnn said.

Janice looked from LuAnn to Tess and back again. She could see she wasn't going to win this one. "Fine."

LuAnn was already crossing the parking lot toward the front door, and Tess was following just a step behind. Reluctantly, Janice went along behind them. They went up the steps and into the lobby for the second time in two days. As they stepped inside, Janice remembered the teller who had turned and disappeared into the back when they'd stepped inside the day before. This time, there was no missing the brown ponytail, and she hadn't had time to run. Brin was standing behind the counter, her mouth open. She was wearing the dark blue blazer that all the tellers wore and had a name tag.

"If you'll excuse me," she said to the customer who was filling out a deposit slip, "I'll be right back." She stepped to the side and gestured for Janice to come toward the counter. "Look, I'm sorry I lied," she said. "I can explain."

"I very much hope so," Janice said.

"I get off at four today. How about I come by the inn then?"

"That would be just fine," Janice said. Part of her wanted to demand an answer here and now, but she supposed that Brin was at work and could get in trouble if she let customers wait too long. "I'll see you at four."

LuAnn's eyebrow was raised, and Tess had her arms crossed over her chest when Janice returned to them.

"We'll see her at four," Janice said. They would have to wait until then to find out what was going on.

When they got home, the kitchen and café were neat, and everything was put away. It was nice to have reliable help, Janice mused. But there were still guest rooms to clean and laundry to do, so before they could watch that security camera footage, they all dove into the chores of running an inn. An hour later, when Janice finally headed up to the fourth floor, Tess was just coming up from the basement, and LuAnn was refilling Huck and Tom's water dish.

"So, shall we take a look at that security footage?" Janice asked.

"Yes. I can't wait to see what's on it." Tess was already heading to the couch. Janice grabbed her laptop from her bedroom and joined her. She inserted the thumb drive, and three videos from the three cameras appeared. She clicked on the first and saw that it was the camera that was pointed at LotzaBurger's drive-through, which wasn't helpful. She closed that and clicked on the second one, which was the camera that was pointed at the parking area at the front of the restaurant. You could easily see the side of the bank in the background.

"There we go," Tess said as Janice enlarged the image. The time stamp in the corner said the footage started at 8:00 a.m. on Saturday. Janice used the little bar at the bottom of the screen to advance the footage to that afternoon.

"Oh, look. Here comes Paul Townsend into LotzaBurger for lunch." Tess laughed. "That diet is working out great for him, isn't it?"

"Don't tell Charlotte," Janice said. This was just after one on Saturday. He must have come over after the bank closed that day. The Thanksgiving Feast planning meeting was just starting at this point. Zelda had said she made the deposit around four that afternoon, so Janice advanced the footage so the time stamp said three thirty, and then she played at fast speed.

They watched as a few people walked up to the ATM and night deposit slot and made deposits or took out cash, but no Zelda. But then, just before four thirty, her car finally appeared. Janice recognized the sporty blue car. It was an older model, but Stuart thought it was cool because it was a stick shift.

"Slow it down," LuAnn said, leaning over the back of the couch to see the screen. Janice slowed it to real time, and they watched as Zelda pulled into a parking spot behind the bank. Janice noted a dark figure in the passenger seat. That had to be Ellen, though it was too blurry and far away to say for sure. Then Zelda emerged from the car holding her keys in one hand, her purse slung over her arm. They watched as she walked toward the bank and stopped in front of the night deposit box. She reached into her purse, took out a black bag, pulled the mailbox-like chute open, and dropped the bag onto it. Then she let the handle go and the chute closed.

"Well, there you go," Janice said. "Proof that Zelda made the deposit after all. We just need to show this to Paul, and we can get the bank to correct the silly error on their end." She frowned. "Although, I always open the chute again to make sure my bag went into the safe."

Tess and LuAnn were quiet.

"What?" Janice said. "This is proof."

"It's proof that she went to the bank," LuAnn conceded.

"And that she put something into the night deposit box," Tess said.

"Well, of course she did." They were being irrational. "The bag was in her hand, and then it's in the box."

"We can't actually say what was in that bag," Tess said. "Someone could have taken the money out before she dropped it in the box."

Janice thought about this. "But Zelda would have noticed," she finally said. "That bank bag was stuffed so full she could hardly zip it. If someone took money out of it, she would have noticed."

"You also can't tell if it was really a bank bag that she deposited," LuAnn said. "From this far away, you can't really tell much of anything."

Janice considered this too. "If she put a bag of any kind into that slot, whether it was full of money or half-full or whatever, the bank would have some record of it," she said. "But Paul said they don't know whether she made the deposit. How could that be?"

"That is a very good question," Tess said. "I suppose there's one possible way."

"What's that?" Janice couldn't see any way.

"It's possible if someone who works at the bank took the bag when they opened the box to enter the deposits on Monday morning." Tess didn't have to say the rest.

"You mean someone like Brin." Janice couldn't believe it. But it was possible, she had to admit. "But we don't know if she was there Monday morning or not. Maybe she only works Wednesdays. For all we know, today could have been her first day at the bank."

But as she said it, Janice remembered seeing the teller with the brown ponytail scurry away as they entered the bank the day before. That had to be Brin, she was sure of it.

"I'm not saying she did it. I'm just saying that she's already lied to you once and didn't seem to be thrilled that we discovered she worked at the bank." Tess paused. "I mean, did you know she worked there?"

"No," Janice said.

"It seems like a strange thing not to mention," LuAnn said. "Given all that's going on."

"I wonder if Zelda knows," Tess said. "She didn't mention it either, which seems strange."

Janice hated to think it was possible. But she didn't see what other option there was. Even if someone had tampered with the deposit before Zelda dropped it in the slot, there would have been something in the safe when they opened it—an empty bag, or some other kind of bag—unless someone inside the bank had intercepted the deposit Monday morning.

"But why would Brin steal the money? She would have known she'd be a suspect, since she lives in the same house as Zelda. And now we know that she works at the bank, that's two strikes against her."

"If she did take the money, she must have been pretty desperate," LuAnn said.

"Agreed," Tess said. "But I'm not sure I'm ready to name her as our number one suspect. Are either of you?"

"No," Janice and LuAnn said in unison.

"But only because I can't make a case for what she would have to gain from getting her mother into so much trouble," LuAnn said.

"I agree." Janice paused to consider all she'd seen and heard regarding Zelda's relationship with her daughter. "The two of them are close. Brin would have to know that her mother would be the first one suspected if the bag and money went missing. That goes against everything I know about her, just as stealing goes against everything I believe is true about her mother."

"I'm sorry to have to say this, Janice," Tess said gently, "but until this investigation is complete, you might need to forget everything you believe is true about Zelda and accept that we can't know everything about a person."

Janice sighed. "I know you're right," she said. "But I just keep thinking about how much Stuart loves her. He's a very good judge of character."

"Of course he is," LuAnn said as she reached across to pat Janice's hand. "We all like her very much and think she is a wonderful person. This isn't about that."

"It's hard to go from wondering what your son's children will look like to wondering if his future fiancée is a thief."

"We know, honey," Tess said. "Either way, we will get through this. And for the record, I would like nothing better than to prove Stuart right. I'm already thinking about what to wear to the wedding."

No one said anything for a moment.

"Brin is coming over here after she gets off work," Janice said. "Let's hope she's able to give us answers then."

"In the meantime, there is another possibility," LuAnn said.

Janice's heart leaped with a spark of hope. "What's that?"

"Maybe someone reached in and took the bag from the deposit box." LuAnn pointed to the screen.

Janice gasped. The footage was running, though none of them had been paying attention to it. But now Janice looked at the screen, and sure enough, there was—Jessica Landry? She was—she was holding the chute open with one hand and trying to stick her arm into the deposit box.

"It looks like we have another suspect," Tess said.

CHAPTER ELEVEN

Janice backed up the footage to before Jessica pulled into the bank parking lot. Then she replayed it slowly, watching the scene advance frame by frame.

"There's the mail truck," Tess said as it parked in the corner of the lot. Jessica stepped out of the driver's side.

"Who's that?" Tess pointed to the other person who stepped out of the passenger side of the van.

Janice squinted, taking in the short figure who followed Jessica across the parking lot. "That must be Hayley, her daughter." She thought back to her conversation with Jessica at the quilt shop the day before. "She told me she switched shifts with a coworker and worked on Saturday. And that Hayley had to write a report for Take Your Child to Work Day, so she came along on her shift."

"That does look like a post office uniform, I guess," LuAnn said.

"She's got the bag," Janice said, pointing to the large mail-bag Jessica had draped across her shoulders. Hayley skipped along behind her. Jessica stopped in front of the night deposit box and the ATM and looked through the bag, then came up holding a handful of envelopes.

"That's a mail slot," Tess said, pointing to a narrow gray band near the deposit box. "I never noticed that before."

"I'm guessing you weren't supposed to," Janice said, and they watched as Jessica lifted the flap and pushed the mail into the building.

"That must be where the vandals put the salmon fillet," LuAnn said.

Tess laughed. "Come on. You have to admit that's pretty funny."

Janice shook her head, but kept her eyes focused on the screen.

Instead of turning to go, Jessica walked over to the ATM. She reached into her bag and pulled out a slim wallet and then took out a bank card. They watched as she inserted her bank card and typed in her pin. Hayley was jumping up and down beside her.

Then they watched as Jessica looked down at her bag.

"Something in the bag has caught her attention," Tess said.

A moment later, Jessica pulled a cell phone out of the bag.

"A phone. Of course," LuAnn said.

Hayley was now trying to climb the wall, using the ATM frame as leverage, but didn't get very far. Jessica was distracted and didn't seem to notice.

Jessica set the mailbag on the ground, put the phone to her ear, and talked while she made her withdrawal. Then she tucked the cash and the card into her wallet and put them both away while she continued to talk.

"If Hayley's a normal kid, she knows this is her chance to experiment a little," Tess said. Hayley had gotten bored of trying to scale the wall and had turned to her mom's mailbag. While Jessica was turned the other way, Hayley pulled out an envelope. When Jessica didn't seem to notice, Hayley took out another and then pushed them both through the mail slot.

"Oh dear. Someone else's mail just ended up inside the bank," LuAnn said.

They watched as Hayley tried it again while her mom chattered away. Then, apparently bored of pushing mail through the mail slot, she grabbed a handful of mail and pulled the night deposit door open. She pushed the handful of mail into the slot and let go of the chute door, which closed presumably with a bang. The noise was enough to get Jessica's attention, and she whipped around and saw her daughter reaching for another handful of mail. She quickly ended the phone call. There was no audio on the footage, but they didn't need to hear what she was saying to understand that Jessica was yelling at her daughter.

Hayley didn't seem all that upset. Jessica went over to the night deposit and pulled it open then reached her arm inside.

"She's not supposed to reach in there," Janice said. "Is she?"

"No, but you're not supposed to put mail in there either. She was probably more worried about getting the mail back than anything else at the moment," LuAnn said.

They watched as Jessica moved her arm around inside the box. But then, before they could see whether she managed to pull anything out, a truck pulled up at the stoplight on the corner and blocked their view of the bank.

"Are you kidding me?" Tess asked. "FedEx, you have to do that now?" There had been cars moving across the screen throughout the video, but none of them had obstructed their view.

"But really," LuAnn said. "It can't be that easy to just reach in and take stuff out of that box. Surely they design those things so you can't do that."

It was more than a minute before the light must have changed, and the truck moved out of the way. By the time the bank came into view once again, Jessica was climbing back into the mail van, Hayley on the passenger side.

"So we don't know if she pulled anything out of that slot or not," LuAnn said. "Mail or otherwise."

"I don't know." Janice shook her head. "Jessica? She seems so honest. Even if she did find the bank bag Zelda had put in there, I just can't see her taking it and pocketing the money."

"But you can't imagine it being Zelda or Brin or Ellen either," Tess pointed out. "And *someone* took that money."

Janice let out a long sigh. She knew Tess was right. But it was so hard to imagine any of those people stealing from the Thanksgiving Feast or the food pantry. But someone had to have done it.

"I guess we'll need to talk to Jessica," Janice said as LuAnn added her name to the suspect list. "But first we need to watch the rest of the footage, to see if anyone tried to take something from the box before Monday morning."

"We don't have time for that right now," LuAnn said. "I've got laundry to get done, and guests are going to start checking in any time now."

"We'll have to find some time later then," Janice said. "We don't want to accuse Jessica of something she didn't do."

Tess went to the office to work on some invoices, LuAnn headed to the basement to do the laundry, and Janice covered the registration desk. She tried to focus on upcoming reservations, but her mind kept drifting to the missing money and all the people who might be responsible for its disappearance.

At ten after four the front door opened, and Janice looked up from her work to see Brin step inside.

"Hi, Janice," she said. She had taken off the blue blazer but still wore dark pants and a white shirt.

"Hello, Brin." Janice led her into the library area and gestured for her to take a seat. She texted Tess and LuAnn and then asked Brin, "Is there anything I can get you to drink? Coffee? Tea? Water?"

"I'm good. Thanks." Brin sat on the couch with her bag at her feet, shifting uncomfortably. A minute later, when Tess and LuAnn had arrived, with them all seated, Janice began.

"When I talked to you this morning, you said you were headed to class," Janice said. "But you went to work at the bank. Why would you lie to me?"

Brin didn't meet her eyes. "I'm sorry I didn't tell you the truth. I wanted to, especially with all you're doing to help my mom. But I couldn't tell. Because no one is supposed to know."

LuAnn tilted her head. "You work as a teller. Everyone who comes into the bank sees your face. You wear a name tag."

Brin sighed. "Well, okay. Really, there's just one person who isn't supposed to know. But my mom never comes into the bank. She just uses the ATM and mobile checking, so I wasn't worried about her catching me."

"But, Brin. Why don't you want your mother to know you have a job?"

Brin hesitated before answering. And then she asked, "What do you know about Mom's financial situation?"

"Just what she told us last Saturday at the meeting," Tess said.

"She told us about her struggle to make ends meet," Janice added. "And that she's really grateful for how hard you've worked to get your scholarship, because she couldn't afford for you to attend such a good school without it."

Brin sighed. "That's about right. My mom has struggled for a while, but she's not one to complain. She just works harder. She raised me on her own, and I know it wasn't easy, so we were both so excited that she's finally getting to see her own dreams start to take off. They were on hold for so long while she was trying to make sure I could pursue my dreams. So when..." She shook her head and wiped the tears now falling. "Sorry. Like I was saying, I... Well, I'm in serious danger of flunking a class this semester. There's so much going on, and I thought I could handle it all. And the material is too hard to understand, and I'm afraid to go to my professor, and...well, anyway. There's no excuse. It's my fault. But it will bring my grade point below the minimum, and I'm going to lose my scholarship."

"Oh, Brin," Janice said. "Why didn't you tell your mother this?"

"Because she would insist on finding a way to pay for my classes, which would mean that she would have to work harder and worry even more. I thought maybe if I could just get a job that—no offense—pays a bit more than the inn, I could be prepared to pay the school back while I bring my grades up next semester and get my scholarship back." She paused to take in a gasp of air and then let it out slowly. "So when my friend Mandy told me there was an opening for a part-time teller at the bank, I thought I'd figured out a way to solve the problem. I moved some classes around so I could be available during the hours the bank needed me, and I've been saving every penny of my paychecks to pay back the college."

"Student loans don't usually come due until after you've graduated and been working for a period of time," LuAnn said. "Why would you have to pay them back now?"

"My scholarship was based on maintaining a certain GPA. When I fell below it, I forfeited the money, and now I have to pay it back to the school." She shrugged. "So not only do I owe for this semester, but I also owe them back for last semester."

"Brin," Janice said gently, "that's a lot for someone your age to take on, especially without help."

"I don't need help," she said. "I can do this. And I don't want my mom to be penalized because of me."

Janice thought through what she said. It just seemed a tad too convenient that Brin had managed to get a job at the very place where her mom's money went missing.

"Do you ever empty the night deposit box?" Janice asked.

"No." Brin shook her head. "They leave that for the more senior employees. I'm new, so I just handle the stuff at the counter. Making deposits, giving change, that kind of thing. But I do know a little about how it works."

"Can you tell us?"

"Sure. First thing in the morning, the shift manager collects the overnight deposits and enters them into the right accounts."

"They do this manually?" Tess asked.

"Well, yes, they type the account number in manually, but the machine counts the cash and reads the checks."

Janice nodded. She had seen the machines that counted out stacks of cash in seconds. It was kind of amazing to watch.

"Were you there on Monday morning, when the weekend deposits were collected?"

"No. I really was at class then," Brin said. "Tara was the one who did the deposits that day, and she swore there was no deposit bag from my mom in the slot."

But they had seen Zelda put the bag into the overnight deposit slot, Janice thought. Which meant that if Tara was right, then Jessica—or someone else—had to have taken the bag from the night deposit box before Monday morning.

"Paul Townsend told us that he's having an auditor look at the records for Monday to make sure there wasn't a mistake in accounting," LuAnn said.

"That's good. I know it'll make Tara feel better to have some-one check that she did it right. I think she feels this cloud over her, like everyone at the bank thinks she did something wrong."

Janice hadn't even thought about how the employees at the bank would be feeling about this whole thing. Tara must be nearly as worried as Zelda was.

"Thanks for stopping by," LuAnn said. "We really do appreciate it."

"Of course." Brin hesitated, twisting her hands in her lap. "I was wondering…"

"Yes?" LuAnn asked, though Janice was pretty sure she knew where Brin was going with this.

"I was hoping, you know, that maybe you wouldn't tell my mom," Brin said. "About the job and the scholarship and all."

"We won't tell her," Janice said. "But you should. This isn't a burden you should feel like you have to carry alone. Your mom will understand. And she might be hurt to know how much you've been keeping from her."

Brin nodded, but didn't commit. Janice wasn't surprised. She probably would have done the same at Brin's age.

Janice walked Brin out to her car and gave her a hug, and then she watched as Brin backed the Jeep out of the parking lot. When she was gone, Janice went back inside and found Tess and LuAnn talking.

"She seems credible," LuAnn said. "And it does explain why she was so secretive. But there's one big problem in believing her story."

"What's that?" Janice asked.

LuAnn let out a sigh. "It's that she was the only one with two strikes against her. Now we have to figure out who our new primary suspect is."

"I'm trying to remind myself that it's good to cross people off if they're not responsible," Janice said with a smile.

"We still need to talk to Jessica Landry," LuAnn said. "To see what she found inside the deposit box."

"If anything," Janice added. "I wish we knew where she lived. We could stop by now."

"It couldn't be that hard to figure out where she lives," LuAnn said. "But maybe it would be better to wait until we see her tomorrow."

"You're probably right," Janice said with a sigh. She would make sure she was around tomorrow at about the time the mail usually came.

"And we need to find out what the auditor at the bank says about the Monday morning deposit," LuAnn said.

"And then there's Ellen," Tess added. "She's still the one with the best opportunity."

"She didn't even get out of the car at the bank," LuAnn said.

"But she could have taken the money from the bank bag at home without Zelda even knowing. And she has a motive. She's trying to get her recording career off the ground. Plus, we know she's got something of a shady past."

"We don't know that," LuAnn said. "Zelda said that she'd had a hard life. She didn't say she'd done anything wrong."

"I suppose you're right," Janice said, chagrined. It wasn't fair to judge Ellen by the circumstances life had handed her. And even if she had done something bad in her past, looking past that and not holding it against her was what grace was all about.

"In any case, I'm going to be looking into her more," Janice said.

"I think you absolutely should," LuAnn said. "Something will turn up."

Janice tried to smile. "This morning Winnie reminded me that God knows where the bank bag is. I'm trying to hold on to that."

"I'm sure He does know where it is," Tess said. "But it sure would be nice if He'd let one of us in on the secret."

CHAPTER TWELVE

November 2, 1859

Long after Jason disappeared down the road, Prudence remained outside. Though she would not journey out of sight of the farmhouse, she could still pace the property in hopes of finding some clue as to where the child came from.

There were no clues, unfortunately, though her silly goose Patience did fall in behind her to enjoy the last rays of the evening sun. When Patience scurried off toward the thicket, Prudence turned back to the porch.

Soon the lamps would be lit. Likely Moses would fret and want his next meal. Likely the baby would be hungry again as well.

Prudence tended to both children and laid them both back in the crib, then she tended to the evening farm chores. Afterwards she ate a solitary dinner, praying for Jason and for his mission.

When Jason finally returned, the night was deep, and he was alone. Prudence greeted him with a smile but held her questions, preferring to allow him to talk first. Rather than speaking, he walked over to where the little ones were and stood over them.

"I made some inquiries," he finally said.

Prudence continued to keep silent. Jason would tell her what he learned in his own time. If he learned anything at all.

CHAPTER THIRTEEN

Janice was wound up and couldn't stop her mind from spinning, so she decided to take a hot bath. Lawrence always said there was nothing like a hot bath to relax the body.

The thought of her husband, whom she missed as much today as the day his life was so suddenly and abruptly ended in that snowstorm, caused her heart to ache. She sighed as she leaned against the sink.

What was it about grief that sometimes made it fresh even when it was months or years in the past?

She stayed in the tub until the water grew cold, but she still had a hard time falling asleep that night. Her mind kept replaying scenes from the day—from talking to Ellen, to reviewing the security footage, to seeing Brin's car in the bank parking lot. Her mind kept spinning, trying to make sense of the clues, but they weren't coming together. If Brin didn't take the money, and Zelda didn't take it, who did? Ellen and Jessica were still possibilities, she knew. They would talk to Jessica tomorrow when she came to bring the mail. But Ellen...Something about the way she had responded to the questions this morning had really bothered Janice. Sure, she was upset to be considered a suspect, but Janice couldn't shake the feeling there was more to it than that. She wanted to talk to Ellen again, but she wasn't at all sure Ellen would agree to that, based on how things had gone today.

Zelda had hinted that Ellen had had a hard childhood. Janice was sure that was part of what was behind her response.

But if Janice knew more about Ellen's past, that might shed light on why she was acting the way she was now.

Janice finally pushed herself up out of bed and took her laptop off her desk. You could learn just about anything about people online these days, she thought. Maybe she'd just take a peek and see what she could learn about Ellen.

She opened a browser and typed in *Ellen Randall* and hit ENTER. The first link that came up was a bio on a website about Christian musicians. Janice read her story and learned that Ellen had started out singing in churches around her home outside of Columbia, Missouri, and had attracted the attention of Clive Clinton, who represented Zelda McLoughlin, among other rising stars. It was the raw emotion in her songs and her ever-present message of redemption that drew listeners to her sound. The article announced that Ellen would be joining Zelda for her upcoming tour and went on to predict a bright career in Christian music for Ellen Randall.

Well, that was great news, but not exactly what Janice had been looking for. The next link was a website Ellen had set up with information about her music and how to contact her to book performances. There were several photographs and a few clips of her songs. She really was good.

She clicked on the next few links, which were locked social media profiles. No doubt her personal accounts, available only to those who were in her circle. That was fine. She didn't expect Ellen to talk about stealing the money on social media anyway.

She clicked through a few more links but didn't find anything useful. She typed in *Ellen Randall Columbia Missouri*. A link came up that appeared to be an article in a local newspaper. TEEN ARRESTED FOR SELLING STOLEN GOODS ONLINE, the headline read. Janice clicked on the link.

A local teenager, identified by police investigators as Ellen Randall of Columbia, was arrested Monday night on charges including grand theft, fraud, and online criminal activity. Randall, a junior at Independence High School, is accused of stealing thousands of dollars' worth of merchandise from local stores, including clothing, electronics, and cosmetics, and reselling them through an online auction site.

"We have surveillance footage of Ms. Randall taking clothing from shelves and stuffing it under her jacket or into her bag," the district attorney said Monday.

A lawyer for Ms. Randall declined comment, but sources close to the case indicate that a plea bargain is in the works for the minor.

Stealing clothing, electronics, and cosmetics and reselling them online. Janice saw how this could work. Ellen would go into a store, sneak an item out, and then sell it through a site like eBay. It was so simple—and so wrong.

Janice clicked back to the main search page and read a couple of follow-up articles where she learned that instead of jail time, Ellen had been sentenced to community service and two years' probation.

Janice tried not to let herself get carried away. Just because Ellen had been convicted of a crime several years ago didn't mean that she was guilty now. Maybe she'd turned over a new leaf. Maybe she'd learned from her mistakes. But it was hard to shake the suspicion that welled up.

She'd need to see what else she could learn about Ellen Randall.

CHAPTER FOURTEEN

The inn phone rang before the first guest had even come downstairs for breakfast Thursday morning. Janice picked it up, hoping something else wasn't wrong. Most phone calls that came this early did not contain good news.

"Wayfarers Inn," Janice said. She'd been filling the sugar bowls and creamers and could smell muffins baking in the kitchen.

"Janice? This is Margaret."

"Hello, Margaret." Margaret Ashworth was the director of the Marietta Historical Society, and they had all gotten to know her since they'd opened the inn. "Is something wrong?"

"Is something wrong?" Margaret said. "I should say so. Didn't you hear about the money for the Thanksgiving Feast that's gone missing?"

"Yes, I heard about that," Janice said. She decided not to add that she and her friends were already looking into what had happened. You had to assume that whatever you told Margaret would end up all over town, and Janice wasn't sure she wanted this spread around widely. "I was just afraid something else was wrong, given the hour."

"I've been up for ages," Margaret said. "I figured I might as well get a move on. I've got a lot of phone calls to make today."

"What can I help you with?" Janice asked.

"I've been looking through the notes from the meetings of the Thanksgiving Feast committee, and I see that you solicited donations from the Sassy Seamstress, Jasmine Tea Shop, Morrison's, Antoinette's, and McHappy's. Is that right?"

"That's right," Janice said. "I also collected donations from Tess, LuAnn, and myself, as well as the inn."

"Great. I'll need you to go back to those places and get them to donate again."

"What?" Janice counted to five before she spoke again. "I'm sorry, I must have misheard you."

"I'm in charge of the committee now that Zelda has stepped down, and I want to make sure we can still pull this thing together in time for Thanksgiving. So I'm asking all the volunteers to go back and get donations from their locations again."

"Zelda stepped down?" How had Janice not heard that?

"Well, all but. I mean, you can't really expect her to continue to lead the committee after what happened, can you?"

That didn't sound like a yes, exactly, but it sure appeared that Margaret had taken control. Janice would find out more about that later. For now, she had other questions.

"It's easy enough to get new checks from the businesses that gave us checks to begin with. Most of them have already put a stop payment on their checks, so there's no danger of doubling up payments on those. But some of the donations were made in cash. We can't ask people to give us more cash, not while we're still trying to figure out what happened to the original donation."

"This is the Thanksgiving Feast, Janice," Margaret said. "People understand how important it is. Who's going to say no to feeding the less fortunate at this time of year?"

Janice, for one, had made her donation in cash, and she wasn't sure her budget would allow for another donation.

"But the bank bag may still be found," she said.

"It may," Margaret said. "And in that case, we'll have a record amount of money in the budget this year. Won't that be something to be proud of?"

Margaret seemed just a little too excited about the prospect, Janice thought.

"I'll see what I can do," she said. It shouldn't be a big deal to get the businesses who'd written checks to write new ones. She could start there anyway.

"And I've brought in the police. They're going to be investigating. So if they come and talk to you, I hope you'll cooperate," Margaret said.

"Of—of course," Janice stuttered. They'd been hoping to solve this before the police got involved. But, she thought, it was a crime that needed to be reported.

"And I'll see you at the meeting on Saturday," Margaret said just before she hung up.

"Who was that?" LuAnn asked.

"Margaret Ashworth."

"Ah."

"She seems to be in charge of the Thanksgiving Feast now."

"I suppose Zelda had to step down, after what happened."

"I guess."

"And Margaret ran it for so many years, she was probably the natural choice," LuAnn said.

"I guess," Janice repeated. Something about it didn't sit right with her. How had Zelda been kicked out as chair so quickly? How had Margaret taken control so fast? "She seemed quite pleased to be in control again."

"Oh, I'm sure," LuAnn said. "She hadn't wanted to step aside to begin with, from what I understand."

"What do you mean?"

"I shouldn't say too much because I don't know the whole story, and I don't want to spread gossip. But when I was talking to Jean Howell at coffee hour after church on Sunday, she said that Margaret hadn't given up the title of committee chair willingly."

"That's interesting," Janice said. "It seems a bit…convenient, doesn't it? That she gets to take over now?"

"I suppose it does," LuAnn said. She leaned back against the counter. "Margaret couldn't have…"

"No." Janice shook her head. "No way." Margaret may not always be the easiest person to work with, but she wouldn't have taken the money so Zelda would have to step down, leaving a leadership gap. Not even she was that devious. "Then again…"

LuAnn was watching her, waiting for her to go on.

It was probably just a coincidence, Janice thought. "Didn't Bev Thornton fracture a bone in her back at the Historical Society?"

"Oh." LuAnn's mouth formed a circle. "You know, I think she did."

"But that has to be a coincidence, right?" Janice said. "How could Margaret have been responsible for that? Bev told me she missed that step up into the room in the back. It's not like Margaret could have engineered that."

"It doesn't seem likely," LuAnn said. "But it sure does seem incredibly lucky that both the new chair and then her replacement had to step down, and then here comes Margaret, waiting in the wings to step in and run things again."

Janice couldn't disagree. "I guess we should do some digging around and see if it's anything more than coincidence."

"I think we should," LuAnn said.

<hr />

For the rest of the morning, Janice tried to keep herself busy with tasks around the inn. Later she planned to go back to the shops where she'd solicited donations previously and ask them to donate again, per Margaret's instructions. But she needed to stick around the inn until the mail came. She started to skim the paper, but the front page read CHRISTIAN SINGER ZELDA MCLOUGHLIN LAST ONE TO SEE MONEY BEFORE IT "DISAPPEARS," so Janice flipped the paper over and got back to work. She dusted the mantel and the bookshelves in the lobby, and she helped Tess wipe down and mop the café while LuAnn checked several guests out and a few others in. She spent some time working on reservations in the office. She was being productive, but she was also determined not to miss Jessica Landry when she came by with the mail, and clearly Tess and LuAnn were feeling the same way.

Janice had told LuAnn and Tess what she'd discovered about Ellen last night, and they had all agreed that they needed to do some more investigating into her actions on Saturday. Her history of theft, coupled with her sour attitude at being questioned, left a lot of doubt in all their minds.

In the meantime, though, Jessica was no doubt on her way with the mail, and they were eager to talk with her.

Janice looked up every time the door opened, but first it was a new set of guests, and then it was a wedding planner who was hosting an event at the inn in the spring, wanting to measure the lobby. Finally, though, the door opened, and Jessica Landry stepped inside, carrying a stack of packages.

"Howdy," she said, closing the door behind her with her foot. The top box started to teeter off the stack. "You've got a lot here today. Are you trying to make sure I get my workout?"

Jessica laughed, and LuAnn rushed forward to take the top box from her.

"Oh, good. It's that special pine-scented potpourri I ordered," she said, setting the box on the front desk. "For use only after Thanksgiving," she added with a wink before Janice could say anything.

"And these are those glasses we ordered to replace the broken ones." Tess took the next largest box from Jessica's arms.

"That's why they're so heavy," Jessica said. "Where should I set this big one?"

Janice had no idea what was in that one, but she pointed to a spot on the floor by the check-in desk. Jessica then reached into her bag and pulled out a stack of envelopes, magazines, and catalogs. Janice held out her hands, and Jessica handed her the pile.

"Phew. You ladies sure keep me in shape," Jessica said.

"We appreciate you," LuAnn said. And then she added, "You know, the strangest thing happened yesterday."

"What's that?" Jessica asked.

"Well, I don't know if you heard about those donations for the Thanksgiving Feast that went missing," LuAnn said.

"Oh yeah, everyone in town is talking about it." Jessica nodded, her eyes wide.

Janice had no doubt everyone in town was talking about it, and she really wanted to know what they were saying. Jessica talked to everybody on her route. She must know everything that went on in this town. But Janice didn't want to encourage gossip, so she bit her tongue.

"What are they saying?" Tess asked. Janice had to smile. That was Tess. Sometimes she just couldn't help herself.

"Oh, you know. Some people think it was that singer who's staying with Zelda that took it. Some think someone in the bank is responsible, but that Paul Townsend doesn't want to admit it. Someone told me an elaborate conspiracy theory involving magnets. But most people seem to think Zelda must have pocketed the money." She glanced at Janice apologetically. "Sorry. I know your son is dating her and all, and Stuart is a fine man. Just, you know, that's what people are saying around town."

It stung to hear her fears realized, but this knowledge didn't exactly come out of the blue. Janice had suspected as much. She knew Zelda was innocent, but there were plenty of people who didn't know her who would be quick to judge based on half-truths and misinformation.

"There are some people who are calling for her to be arrested," Jessica said.

Janice gasped. "Really? But they don't have any evidence that she's responsible, do they?"

"Not that I heard about." She reached out and patted Janice's arm. "Now, don't you worry. Obviously the police don't agree, or they would have done something about it. There's no need to worry about idle gossip. But you wanted to hear what I've been hearing, and that's the scuttlebutt."

Janice blew out a breath. She hated hearing it. Her heart ached for Zelda. But she held on to the fact that Zelda hadn't been arrested, or even anything close.

"What do you think happened?" Tess asked Jessica.

"I don't know." Jessica hitched her bag up on her shoulder. "It's hard to imagine anyone in this town doing something like that. Taking money that's supposed to go to feed people who can't afford a Thanksgiving meal?" She shook her head. "It's nuts."

"It certainly is," LuAnn said. "And because Zelda is a friend of ours, we've been helping her look into the missing money."

"Oh, good. I was hoping you were. You ladies are better at solving this kind of thing than the police any day."

"I don't know about that," Janice said, though secretly she was flattered by the praise.

"The thing is, we were reviewing the security camera footage from outside LotzaBurger yesterday," LuAnn said.

"Oh, my goodness. Hayley loves that place."

"You can see the bank from one of their security cameras," LuAnn continued, "and we saw the strangest thing on the footage from Saturday."

Janice could tell the very moment Jessica figured out what they were going to tell her. Her mouth formed an *O*, and she sucked in a breath.

"Oh, dear. Don't tell me they caught that." she said.

"Why don't you tell us what you think the cameras caught?" Tess asked.

"Only one of the most embarrassing parenting fails of my life." Jessica took off her hat and ran her fingers through her hair. "I should have thought about the cameras. I was just thinking I had to get that mail back, stat."

"You had your daughter with you on Saturday," LuAnn prompted.

"That's right. My coworker Hank had a wedding to go to, so we swapped shifts," Jessica said. "Hayley had to write a report about what her parents do and shadow one of us for the day. Well, Jake works in a lumber mill, so that didn't really seem like the safest place to take Hayley, so I said she could tag along with me for the day. It seemed like a simple enough thing. Oh, boy. I had no idea what I was setting myself up for."

"Hayley gave you a run for your money, huh?" Janice laughed.

"She confirmed that we made the right decision to stop at one child." Jessica laughed too. "She spent half the day resorting the mail by color, which meant I had to go back and redo it all. And she kept opening letters and reading them. I don't know how many times I told her that's a felony, but she didn't care."

"Perhaps she doesn't know what a felony is," Tess suggested.

"You're probably right," Jessica said. "But it shouldn't matter. I told her to stop, and she didn't. It took twice as long to deliver the mail as it should have, and it was an unfamiliar route to boot, so that only slowed things down more. The bank was one of my last stops for the day, and by the time we got there, I'd had it. Which, I recognize now, only encouraged her further."

"And then you got a phone call," LuAnn said.

"Exactly. That's when she started putting mail into the bank's mail slot and the night deposit box. I was mortified. Well, I knew I wasn't going to be able to get the ones she'd put through the mail slot back, but I thought I might be able to get the ones she'd stuck in the night deposit. So that's no doubt what caught your attention on the security footage, right?"

Janice nodded. "Were you…" How did Janice phrase this carefully? "Did you worry at all about the consequences of reaching into the bank's deposit box?"

"In other words, did you realize it's a felony?" Tess said.

"No." Jessica laughed. "I probably should have thought about that. But I was so concerned about getting the mail back right away that I didn't stop to worry about the consequences at all."

"Were you able to get anything out of the box?" Janice asked.

"No," Jessica said. "I thought it might be just a big box inside, but it's more like one of those mailboxes where it drops your deposit but you can't reach in. I tried pretty hard though, and have the scars to prove it."

She pulled up her sleeve and showed them the bandage Janice had seen on her arm on Wednesday.

"How did you do that?" LuAnn asked.

"I scraped it on the inside of the box somehow. Must have been a loose screw or something. I don't know exactly how it happened. I'm a total klutz, so naturally if there was a way to get injured, I'd find it."

"That's terrible," Tess said. "It looks serious."

"Nah." Jessica shook her head. "I was afraid it would need stitches at first, but the doctor just bandaged it up."

Janice tried to picture the deposit box. How could a scrape like that happen? She wasn't sure where the metal would have come from to scrape Jessica's arm. Then again, she certainly hadn't ever studied the inside of a deposit box.

"So you didn't get your mail back?" Tess said.

"Not that day. I had to go talk to Paul Townsend Monday morning and swear him to secrecy. He was very understanding. He gave me the mail back, and I gave it to Hank to deliver on Monday."

"Did you find anything else when you tried to reach into the deposit box?" Tess asked.

Jessica tilted her head. "Nothing other than the metal. Why?"

They had discussed this ahead of time. If Jessica asked why they were anxious to find out about her reaching into the deposit box, they were going to tell her the truth. But now, Janice hesitated to get it out. There was no good way to say this without making it sound like they were accusing her.

"It's just that the bank doesn't have any record of Zelda depositing the money," LuAnn said carefully. "But we can see on the security footage that she did. So we were hoping you might be able to verify that it was there when you reached in."

"Oh. I see." She shook her head. "I'm afraid I can't help you there. All I felt was the jagged edges of a piece of metal." She held her arm out again. "Everything else seems to have already been where I couldn't reach it."

If she saw what they were really asking, she did a good job of hiding it.

"Anyway, I should probably get going. With the holidays coming up, I've already noticed an uptick in the amount of mail being sent out, so it's taking me longer than usual to get through my rounds."

"In that case, we appreciate you stopping in to chat even more," LuAnn said.

"And keep us posted on the scuttlebutt," Tess called.

Jessica laughed and promised she would as she headed out.

"The scuttlebutt?" Janice said as the door closed behind her.

"That's what she called it," Tess said, shrugging. "Come on, don't you want to know what people are saying about all this?"

"I want to know the truth about what happened to that money," Janice said, shaking her head. "And after talking to her, I don't really believe Jessica Landry took it."

"No, sadly, I don't either," Tess said. "I mean, I'm not sad she didn't steal the money. I like her and would have hated to have to get to know a new mail carrier when she went to prison."

LuAnn was shaking her head and grinning.

"But I am sad that it seems we have to cross another name off the suspect list."

"I agree," Janice said with a sigh.

She started to pick up the box of glasses so she could take it to the kitchen, but her phone rang, so she stopped and dug it out of her pocket. *Stuart.*

"Hi there," she said, holding the phone to her ear. She moved into the empty café so she wouldn't bother Tess and LuAnn. "How are you?"

"I'm all right," he said.

"You sound tired."

"I'm sure you know Margaret called the police and reported the money stolen."

"I heard. I also heard Zelda stepped down as chair of the committee."

"'Stepped down' might not be the exact phrase I would use," Stuart said.

"You mean she was asked to step down."

"Not in so many words, but yes. And if that wasn't bad enough, Zelda just spent several hours talking to the police.

They seem to see her as the primary suspect. Which, you know, makes some sense, I guess. But I know she didn't do it. So I sat in with her while they talked to her."

"Oh, dear." That sounded like an ordeal. He was a good man for doing that for her. And yet... "Shouldn't a lawyer have been the one to sit with her? If the police are interviewing her?"

Stuart let out a long breath. "I tried to convince her of that, but Zelda says she doesn't need a lawyer, because she has nothing to hide."

"I don't know if that's the best strategy," Janice said.

"I agree with you. But what can I do? I can't force her. I figured having me there was better than having her face them alone."

"I suppose." Janice couldn't believe it. If Zelda was being questioned by the police, things really were getting serious. "Did they talk to anyone else in the household?"

"Yes. They interviewed Ellen and Brin too, but only for a short time."

"But they both seem more likely to be suspects than Zelda does," Janice said.

"That's not much consolation considering that's her daughter and the young woman she's supposed to be looking out for."

"No," Janice said. "I suppose it's not."

"The bigger problem is that there's a morals clause in her contract that will be activated if she's arrested. If that happens, the contract will be canceled, as well as the tour, and she'll have to pay back all the money the label has spent making her album."

"In that case, let's hope she did steal the money. That'll make it a whole lot easier to pay it back." When he didn't laugh, she added, "That was a joke."

"I know it was. I'm just not in the mood to laugh right now."

"I'm sorry, honey."

"It's all right. You're not the problem." He sighed. "Anyway, the reason I'm calling is that I was hoping I could ask a huge favor."

"What's that?"

"Well, Ellen isn't feeling particularly warm toward Zelda at the moment. Not since we searched her room and the police questioned her."

"I don't get the sense she feels particularly warm toward anyone. But I'm not sure that's a recent development."

"Ma. That's not helpful."

"I'm sorry." She knew it didn't help things when she was snarky.

"Anyway, things have been a little...tense over at Zelda's. We were thinking giving Ellen a little bit of space would be helpful. So we were wondering if there was any chance..."

Janice saw where this was going.

"You want to know if she can stay here for a while?"

"Not for very long. A few days, maybe. Just long enough for things to settle down."

The inn was busy, but it wasn't full. They had a few rooms available for the next few days.

"Are we supposed to babysit her?"

"No. Nothing like that. We just need to give her a bit of space from...all this."

Janice understood exactly what he meant by "all this."

"I'll need to talk to LuAnn and Tess," she said.

"Of course."

"Will her manager be okay with this arrangement? I got the sense he was really invested in having Zelda mentor Ellen."

"Given the situation, it seems that Clive is fine with it."

Did Janice want Ellen here, given what she knew of her past? And the likelihood that she was behind the theft? She would need to pray about it. But she couldn't tell Stuart that.

"Okay. In that case, let me check in with the others, and I'll let you know." It was the truth, or at least part of it.

"Thanks, Ma."

"No problem. And Stuart?"

"Yes, Ma?"

"I love you."

"I love you too."

Janice ended the call and headed back to the lobby, where Tess and Janice were chatting by the check-in desk.

"Is everything okay?" Tess asked.

"Yes, I guess so." She explained about the police questioning Zelda and about the tension between Zelda and Ellen. "Stuart was wondering if we could put Ellen up here for a few days, to give the air a bit of time to clear."

"I don't see why not." LuAnn looked down at the tablet they kept at the check-in desk. "It looks like Apples and Cinnamon is available for the next few days."

"Are you sure?" Janice asked.

"We have the room, and if it would help Zelda, I don't see why not."

"What about..." Janice almost hated to bring it up, in case they'd forgotten.

"What about the fact that she might be the thief?" LuAnn asked.

"And the fact that she's been convicted of grand theft in the past?" Tess added.

"Yeah. What about all that?"

"I say it's better for her to be under our roof in that case," Tess said. "So we can keep an eye on her."

"I agree," LuAnn said. "If she knows where that money is, having her stay here will make it even easier to get it out of her."

"You guys aren't worried that she'll..."

"Steal from us?" LuAnn asked.

Janice nodded.

"I suppose it's a risk. But one that we'll have to live with," Tess said.

"You guys are the best," Janice said. "I don't know how to thank you."

"The best way to thank us will be solving this mystery so we can get this Thanksgiving dinner back on track," Tess said.

"And so Zelda can put this all behind her, and Stuart can put that ring on her finger," LuAnn said.

Janice smiled, imagining that day. "That will be nice, won't it?"

"Go give Stuart a call," LuAnn said.

"And then we have some donations to solicit," Tess said.

"You'll come with me?" Janice asked.

"Of course." Tess nodded. "It's better than having Margaret come after me."

CHAPTER FIFTEEN

November 2, 1859

Jason squatted down and studied the sleeping babies. Finally, he scooped up the little girl and stood. Cradling her in his arms, he looked down at the baby girl.

"There is a friend to our cause who has recently come to work at the orphanage."

The orphanage? Surely not. This child had to have a family out there somewhere. And even if she did not, Prudence could…Prudence did want her.

"John Paige, he is called," Jason continued. "I do not believe thee has met him."

"I have not," she managed. He could not be thinking of sending this child to an orphanage. The stories she'd heard about what went on there—it was unthinkable.

"He speaks fondly of Miss Fay and says she treats the children as if they are her own."

Prudence knew this was true, but townspeople said otherwise.

"I have heard the rumors too," Jason said. "But John tells me they are not true. Not since Miss Fay took over last May. He says she truly cares for the children."

Prudence wanted to believe him. She hoped it was true. She had heard that Catherine Fay had angered many in town with her insistence that the children in her care be allowed to attend school in Marietta. Rather than let the bullies win, Miss Fay marched down to the courthouse and demanded to be named guardian of all nine of the orphan children. It was possible the circumstances of the home had changed since her arrival.

Her tactic had worked, and the children were now being properly educated and treated as equals to the others who attended alongside them. But that didn't mean this child would be safe there. Would be cared for.

Finding her a family would be preferable.

The little girl let out a soft sigh, coaxing a smile from Jason. "According to John, someone asked about a child a few days ago. A babe newly born." Jason looked at Prudence. "A female child. With dark eyes and hair, but light skin."

Prudence lowered herself to the nearest chair. "Who was asking?"

Jason knew what she meant. Was this family or owner?

"John aims to find out."

She let out the breath she had been holding. "All right."

He returned the little one to her spot beside Moses and then stepped around the babies to kneel beside Prudence.

"Until we know for certain, she will remain with us." He looked into her eyes. "But, Prudence, do not get too attached. She must leave here."

Prudence buried her face in his shoulder. Tears filled her eyes and prevented her from speaking.

"I am a father," he whispered. "And a father will always do what is best for his child, even when it is hard. She is safe with us for now."

"Yes," Prudence managed. "She is."

"For now," he warned again. "But not for long. For all the reasons thee has likely already considered, she must find her home very soon."

Chapter Sixteen

Janice called Stuart back, and he promised that someone would bring Ellen by that afternoon. Janice took that to mean that Ellen's car was still in the shop. In the meantime, Janice and Tess bundled up in their heavy wool coats and set out for Morrison's Book Shop. A few snow flurries twisted around them as they crunched their way through the fallen leaves along Front Street. They stepped inside the bookshop and let the door fall closed behind them.

"Hello there." Tama Steele looked up from the book she was reading behind the cash register. She had dark-framed glasses and peroxide blond hair with dark roots, but something told Janice that was the look she was going for. Tama couldn't have been more than thirty, but she had opened this thriving bookstore and was running it while raising a young son alone. "How's it going today?" she greeted them.

"Pretty good," Janice said. "We were—"

She turned to Tess, but she had already wandered off to look at a display of novels that were advertised as great Christmas presents.

Too early, she thought. But Tess was already taking a book from the stack.

"We were hoping to bother you again about that donation for the Thanksgiving Feast," Janice said apologetically. "I know you canceled the check you wrote last week, and well, I was wondering if you could be convinced to consider writing a new one."

Tama laughed. "I would more than consider it. I was planning on it." She climbed down from the stool. "Hang on a minute. I'll go get one written."

"That would be great, thanks."

"Of course. I'm just sorry for all the problems. I sure hope the meal can still happen. Milo had so much fun last year, and it's such a nice tradition."

Tama's four-year-old son Milo was a sweet kid with blond hair and big glasses just like his mom's.

"We're trying to do everything we can to make sure it happens," Janice said. While Tama walked to the back, Janice looked around, taking in the blond wood shelves and the plain white walls. It was bright and cheerful, and Janice found herself drawn to a shelf of mysteries.

A few minutes later, Tama returned with a check in her hand, and Janice thanked her again before putting it in a manila envelope she'd brought along to gather the donations.

"Ready?" She turned to find Tess's nose buried in a book with a picture of a girl standing in a river on the cover.

"I'll take this one," Tess said. "It's a Christmas present for myself."

Tama rang up her purchase, and then they headed off to McHappys, where they collected another check and a donut apiece. Then they hit up the Sassy Seamstress and Jasmine Tea Shop, and finally they stepped inside Antoinette's Closet.

"Hi there." Emma Carpenter was setting a vintage aluminum Christmas tree in the front window.

"Oh, my." Janice shook her head as the door closed behind her. "I haven't seen one of those in years."

"Oh, my goodness. We had one of those when I was a kid." Tess laughed. "It had an electric light wheel that changed the color of the tree."

"Got it right here." Emma held up a black box with a colored lens on the front. "Are you ladies interested? It's for sale."

"Oh, dear. I think LuAnn would kill us," Tess said with a laugh.

"Sadly, I don't think it exactly matches the aesthetic we're going for," Janice said.

"Suit yourself." Emma shrugged and stepped out of the window. "So what can I do for you ladies? I've got some gorgeous party dresses here. Going to a holiday soiree?" She gestured toward the back wall, where a strapless black sequin dress hung next to a gold lamé miniskirt. Janice and Tess burst out laughing.

"Only if you want us to scare the neighbors," Tess said.

"I think my lamé miniskirt days are past, unfortunately," Janice said. "Actually, we're here to ask you about your donation to the Thanksgiving Feast." They explained what they were doing, and Emma went to the counter to write a check.

When she returned, Tess was looking at a display of silk scarves in a sixties-era suitcase.

"There are some pretty ones in there," Emma said. "And they're going like hotcakes."

"Really?" Emma was right, there were some pretty scarves in here. Janice eyed one in a green and blue paisley pattern.

"Sort of." Emma made a face. "What I mean is, there seems to be fewer of them than there were before. Somehow like half the scarves vanished the other day, along with a jean jacket and a pair of shoes."

"What?" Janice froze.

"Yeah, it was the weirdest thing. It was really busy in here on Sunday because I was having a two-for-one sale, and there were people in and out all day. I was busy ringing up sales and helping customers and whatnot. Just slammed. It was only when I started to clean up and shut down for the evening that I realized they were missing. I went back over my receipts for the day, but I didn't find any record of them. They'd somehow vanished."

"Vanished?" Tess asked.

"Well, more likely, someone stuck them in their bag and walked out with them." Emma shrugged. "I suppose I'm lucky it hasn't happened before."

The hairs on the back of Janice's neck stood up.

There was no reason to believe...just because it sounded a bit like...

"Were most of the customers that came in here people you know?" Tess asked. She suspected the same thing, then.

"Yeah. For the most part, I either recognized them or knew them from town. We get a lot of repeat customers, that kind of thing. But there were some people I didn't know too."

Janice turned and looked up at the ceiling. "You don't have security cameras in here?"

"No. I never thought I needed them. And having them installed would probably cost more than the cost of the goods stolen. But it is frustrating."

Janice looked at Tess, who was nodding. "Of the people who came in that you didn't know, would you be able to recognize them again?"

"Probably," Emma said. "I mean, I don't know if I could remember anything about them now, but I might be able to if I saw a picture of them."

They didn't have any reason to assume that Ellen was one of the people who had come in here, Janice knew. Just because she'd been shopping for clothes at Olive Saturday and walked away without buying anything didn't mean she had come in here and stolen things. But the collection of things taken seemed so random—a jacket, shoes, and silk scarves? Almost as if someone had just grabbed a handful of things without really caring what it was...because they weren't going to wear any of it anyway?

Janice hesitated. It wasn't fair to assume Ellen had anything to do with this. But then, what did it hurt to find out?

"Hold on one second," she said and pulled her phone out of her purse. She opened a browser window and typed the name *Ellen Randolph*. Then she pulled up Ellen's webpage, the one she'd looked over the night before, and pulled up a picture of her.

"Is she one of the people who came in on Saturday?"

"Yeah. She was here." Emma's long black hair swept her shoulders as she nodded.

"You're sure?"

"Yep. She was with some other girl. Brown hair, I think?"

That had to be Brin, Janice guessed.

"She looked around for a while, but she didn't buy anything." Emma shrugged. "Who is she?"

"She's just someone we know," Tess said.

They said goodbye on the way out the door. As they walked down the sidewalk, Tess finally broke the silence. "I guess it doesn't prove anything, does it?"

Janice sighed. "I think the only thing it proves is we have to keep our eyes open. We aren't the only ones in the inn that Ellen could steal from."

"But do you really think it was Ellen who stole from Emma's store?" Tess asked as they walked to the Marietta Historical Society. They'd decided that after what had already happened, they didn't want to be responsible for holding on to the new set of donations they'd solicited, so they planned to drop them off with Margaret for safekeeping. The snowflakes had stopped, but the wind was bitterly cold, and Janice pulled her hat down over her brow.

"I don't know," she said. "It sure seems a bit too similar for it not to be related to the thefts she was convicted of. But obviously we can't say one way or the other."

"That's the most frustrating thing about this whole situation," Tess said. "We just don't know anything for sure."

"We know that the Lord is in control," Janice said. "And that's not nothing."

"I know you're right, but that doesn't make it feel any less frustrating," Tess said.

Janice understood the feeling, but she hated to admit it. A few minutes later, they pushed open the door of the Marietta Historical Society and stepped inside. The front room held a display featuring information about General Rufus Putnam, the man credited with first settling the town. Tess led Janice back to one of the rear rooms, where they found Margaret Ashworth huddled over a desk.

"Hello, Margaret," Janice said.

"There you are," Margaret said, as if she'd summoned them. Janice looked at Tess. Margaret hadn't even known they were coming. "How is it going with the donations?"

"That's actually why we've come," Janice said. "We were able to get some of the business owners to write new checks to replace the ones that disappeared. And we're hoping we could give them to you now so we don't have to be responsible for them."

"That's wise," Margaret said. "Given your connection to Zelda, I think that makes perfect sense. I'd be happy to store them in the safe here at the museum until Saturday."

Janice felt anger rise up in her. How dare she accuse Zelda—but she bit back the angry response, knowing it wouldn't help and instead said, "Thank you."

They handed Margaret the checks they'd collected, and she set them in a neat pile on the desk.

"We will have to work harder than any other year to make this meal happen this time, but now that we've got strong leadership in place, I feel confident we can do it." Margaret peered at them through her big glasses.

"Yes," Tess said uncertainly. "We all hope so."

"And as I told you, I've called the police in to investigate the missing money. It's not exactly a piddly sum, so it wasn't something that could be left to amateurs. I hope you understand."

Janice hated to admit that she did understand. She just didn't like it.

"I would have thought you would be enjoying the break this year," she said.

"I was looking forward to not rushing around and giving up my whole Thanksgiving managing deliveries and such," Margaret said. "Being the chair of the committee is such a big job, you know. And one that takes a lot of experience to pull off successfully. But I'm willing to step in and save the event, since there is such a desperate need this year."

"That's wonderful," Tess said flatly. "It's unfortunate that we've already gone through two committee chairs this year."

"It's terrible, isn't it?" Margaret said. "Like I said, I was happy to step in, but it does show a real vacuum of reliable leadership in this town."

"I'm curious," Janice said. She tried to make her voice seem as neutral and unconcerned as possible. "Why didn't you volunteer to be the chairwoman in the beginning this year?"

Margaret waited just a moment too long before answering, and the way she flicked her eyes down before answering... Janice wasn't sure whether she could trust whatever Margaret was about to say.

"Like I said, it's a huge job, and you spend all of Thanksgiving running around. I was looking forward to a calmer holiday this year."

"But with all your experience...Were you kind of disappointed to let Bev take over this year?"

"Certainly not." This time, the words came out a bit too quickly. "I met with Bev and told her everything I know, and I was sure she would do fine."

There was something Margaret wasn't saying. Janice decided to keep asking questions to see if she could get to whatever it was.

"I missed the meeting where she was elected," Janice said. "Was it a unanimous vote?"

"No." Margaret's response was just a bit too forceful. "There were those who were pushing to have me run the event again. But I was happy to step aside. Time to get some new blood in here, and all that."

Margaret was trying hard to convince them...and maybe herself, Janice realized.

"It must have been so disappointing when Bev fell and had to step down," Tess said. And then, as if she'd just thought of it, "Actually, didn't that happen here?"

"Yes, she fell right in the back room. Tripped over the step. It was just awful. I was so worried she was going to sue. You know how people are these days. They stub a toe on your property and want to sue you."

Bev had done more than stub her toe. She'd fractured a bone in her back. But it wouldn't help to point that out now.

"How did it happen? Did you see her fall?" Janice was probing to see whether there was any way Margaret could have… helped things along.

"No. I was in here." Margaret shook her head. "Of course I came running and helped however I could. It was terrible. Totally put me behind in my work on the new display."

"It must have been awful for Bev too," Tess said. Janice could see how hard she was fighting to keep her voice neutral. "She must have been really looking forward to chairing the committee."

"Oh yes, of course," Margaret said. "I offered to take over at that point, but Zelda wanted to have a go at it, so who was I to get in her way." There was something in her face that Janice couldn't read.

"Well, thankfully you've got it under control now," Tess said breezily.

"And hopefully, with this new set of donations, we're on our way to making the event happen," Janice said.

"Thank you for your work," Margaret said. "It's a team effort."

Janice and Tess turned to go. Janice was extra careful as she stepped out the door, and then she and Tess started walking back toward the inn.

"She did not want to step down as committee chair," Tess said.

"No. Not at all. That was all too clear," Janice agreed.

"Do you think she could have had anything to do with the money going missing?"

"I don't know." Janice pulled her scarf a bit tighter against the bitter wind. "It does seem to be a pretty big coincidence that Bev Thornton managed to hurt herself badly enough to take herself out of commission at the historical society. But if Margaret was at the far end of the museum when it happened, I can't see how she could have been responsible for that."

"And then, how would she have taken the money from Zelda?"

"And doesn't it all seem like a long way to go to get back her spot as committee chair?" Janice asked. "I can see her being upset that someone else was appointed this year, but are we seriously considering the idea that she could have been responsible for Bev breaking her back, and then framing Zelda for grand theft just to get her role back?"

"It does sound far-fetched," Tess agreed. "Still, given how she responded to our questions, I'm not sure I'm willing to rule her out entirely yet."

"Neither am I," Janice said.

"Which means we're back to where we started," Tess said. "We don't know anything about this case for sure."

"I know one thing for sure," Janice said.

"What's that?"

"We are way overdue for lunch." Janice stopped walking. "I'm starving. Again."

Tess gave her a sidelong glance. "Want to hit up Lotz-aBurger again?"

"No thanks." Janice patted her belly. "I mean, yes, I want to, obviously. But I'd better not. With the holidays coming up, I'd better not splurge too often now."

"I suppose you're right," Tess said. "Winnie was making broccoli cheddar soup when we left."

"Ooh...That'll hit the spot." They hurried home, and after warm, filling bowls of soup, Janice cleaned a couple of guest rooms and then went into Apples and Cinnamon to make sure it was ready for Ellen when she arrived.

She had just finished fluffing the pillows when a blue Jeep pulled into the driveway. Brin. Janice hurried downstairs to meet them and found Ellen and Brin already chatting with LuAnn and Tess in the lobby.

"We hope you'll make yourself at home," LuAnn was saying. "Help yourself to meals and whatever you need."

After her trip to Antoinette's Closet, Janice wanted to put a few parameters on that freedom but kept her mouth shut.

Brin was looking around, taking in the antique furniture and the carved mantel. "I will never get over how beautiful this place is," she said. "I can't believe you get to live here, Ellen."

Ellen scowled and rolled her eyes. Janice had to admit, it wasn't the most sensitive thing Brin could have said.

"And did my mom tell you there are Underground Railroad tunnels under here? That's still so amazing to me," Brin continued.

"Would you like to take a look?" LuAnn asked. LuAnn loved history and was always proud to show off the entrance to the tunnel.

"That would be amazing."

"Ellen? Would you like to come too?" LuAnn asked.

Janice could hardly see Ellen's eyes beneath her bangs, but she made out the look of disdain on her face.

"Why don't we go get your stuff and bring it in?" Tess asked quickly. LuAnn led Brin to the stairs to look at the tunnels, and Janice and Tess went with Ellen to the parking lot. Tess opened the rear door, and Ellen leaned in to gather her bags. Janice opened the passenger side door and saw the black guitar case that was leaning against the seat. It was an awkward shape, and Janice wanted to handle the instrument very carefully, so she bent forward and found the handle. Then she spotted something under the passenger seat. Something black. Something that looked remarkably like a bank bag.

Janice set the guitar down on the pavement and reached under the seat and pulled the bag out. It was indeed a bank bag, she saw. It looked just like the one that had disappeared on Saturday.

Janice unzipped it slowly. It was full of cash.

CHAPTER SEVENTEEN

A few minutes later they were all standing in the lobby. The three innkeepers were standing together, and Brin and Ellen were facing them. Janice held the bank bag while Brin explained that this was not the same bank bag that her mom had deposited Saturday evening.

"It's a different bag, I promise," Brin said. She looked from one of them to the other as if desperate for them to believe her. "Let me explain."

Janice wanted to shout that of course it couldn't be a different bag, that she'd trusted her, that Brin had betrayed that trust. That she was about to become her grandmother, and she couldn't even trust her. But instead, she forced herself to say calmly, "Why don't you explain it to us, then?"

Ellen had her arms crossed over her chest. A hint of a smile said she was enjoying this.

"You know I took that job at the bank," Brin said. They all nodded. "That's where I got the bag. I've been saving the money I earn, every penny, so I can pay the college back. I wanted to keep it somewhere where I wouldn't be tempted to spend it. Where it wouldn't be easy to get to."

"And you didn't think to keep it, in, say, I don't know, a . . . *bank*?" Tess asked.

Ellen laughed. Janice had to admit, it was a very good question. A bank would have been the logical place to keep the money.

"I thought about that," Brin said. "Of course. But because I work at the bank, it's not like it would be hard to get my hands on it there. So I decided to keep it somewhere else. Someplace safe."

"Yeah, 'cause everyone knows no one ever steals anything out of cars." Ellen sure had a gift for sarcasm.

While Janice didn't appreciate her attitude, she had a point.

"Ellen's right. Cars get broken into all the time. You're never supposed to leave anything valuable in the car," LuAnn said.

"Look, I know people say that. But honestly, have you seen my car? No one looks at a lot full of cars and decides mine is the one with the valuable stuff inside. And it was well hidden. I didn't leave it in the glove compartment or anywhere obvious like that. It was tucked up under the seat in an unmarked bag. No one would have thought to look there."

"But what if the whole car had been stolen?" Tess said.

Brin lifted her shoulder. "Again, I wasn't really worried about that. Most thieves would be going for a nicer car than mine."

"Perhaps not all thieves are that picky," LuAnn said.

If Brin had left the money in her car, that explained why Stuart and Zelda hadn't uncovered it when they'd searched her bedroom. Which seemed just a tad bit too convenient, Janice thought. But there was something else that was bothering her. "Doesn't the bank pay you by check?"

"Yes, and then I cash it," Brin said.

"So...wait." This didn't make sense. "The bank pays you by check. And then, instead of just depositing the check into the bank, where it would be safe, you cash it and then put the cash inside your car, which you use every day, so you won't spend it?"

"Now that you say it like that, it sounds like a bad plan," Brin said. "But I never thought of it like that. I just thought, out of sight, out of mind. And, look, it's not like banks are even all that safe. I know I work there so I'm supposed to say they're totally safe and all that, but honestly, the money my mom deposited Saturday vanished from the bank, so how safe are they, really?"

Her logic was flimsy at best. Janice could tell by looking at Tess's and LuAnn's faces that they were having a hard time believing her too. Then again, Brin was nineteen and living a very unpredictable life. She'd watched her mom struggle with money and hadn't had great financial role models. Was it possible she was telling the truth?

Tess let out a sigh and looked at LuAnn and Janice. "Do we know how much was in the bank bag Zelda lost track of Saturday?"

"I don't know," Janice said. "Even if I did, I wouldn't know how much was in checks and how much was cash. We'd have to ask Zelda for the breakdown."

She saw what Tess was getting at. The bag they'd found in Brin's car contained only cash. If Brin had taken the bank bag from her mom, she likely would have gotten rid of the checks and just kept the cash. So they needed to find out whether the amount of cash in this bank bag matched the amount that had been in the one Zelda lost.

"I'll give her a call," Janice said.

"You can't call my mom." Brin's face had gone white. Because she was afraid her mom would guess the truth of where the money in that bag had come from? "She'll want to know where I got it, and I'll have to tell her about the job and about losing my scholarship, and she's already been through so much..." Her voice trailed off as she glanced at Ellen. Ellen's eyes were wide, but she didn't say anything.

She was right about that, Janice knew. Starting way back in high school. Zelda had been at a party when someone had slipped something in her drink, and Brin was the result of what happened next. Zelda had been strong and brave then and had been a wonderful mother to Brin ever since that awful night. She wouldn't be able to just let Brin figure this out on her own. It wasn't in her nature.

"I don't see what other option we have," Tess said. "We need to find out how much cash was in that bank bag to know for sure if this is the same one."

"Besides," Janice said softly, "it's probably time for you to tell your mom the truth about your scholarship. It's not fair to you or to her to keep that from her."

Brin looked down at the floor but didn't say anything.

"Why don't we hold on to this, just in case," Janice said, still holding the bank bag. "We'll put it in the safe and won't take anything out. Assuming everything is aboveboard, we'll hand it back to you once we get this all squared away." And if it wasn't aboveboard, well…they'd cross that bridge when they came to it.

Brin didn't seem to see any other option, because she didn't argue. She just turned and headed out. "Call me when you have an answer," she said as she walked out the door.

The three innkeepers were left staring at each other. So many thoughts flooded Janice's mind—what if Brin was telling the truth? What if she wasn't? Could she possibly have stolen the money from her mom after all? Why would she do that?

Ellen cleared her throat, and they all turned to her. Janice had momentarily forgotten she was there.

"Can I head up to my room?" she asked.

"Of course." Janice let out a breath. "Let's get you settled in."

Tess locked the bank bag in the safe, and LuAnn headed upstairs to call Zelda. Janice picked up Ellen's guitar, Ellen took her bags, and they rode the elevator together to the third floor.

"Not bad," Ellen said as she walked into the room, which was decorated in reds and browns. It was one of the smaller rooms, and it looked out over the yard at the back of the inn instead of the river, but it had a desk and a closet and a private bath, and Ellen nodded approvingly. "This will work."

Janice decided to take that as a compliment and helped Ellen get her things settled in the closet before she reminded her to help herself to breakfast and lunch in the café. Ellen thanked her, and Janice went upstairs, where she found LuAnn and Tess in their kitchen. LuAnn was chopping onions, and Tess stood on the other side of the counter talking to her.

"It's crazy. It's totally unbelievable that she just happened to have a bank bag full of cash in her car while we're looking for, I don't know, a bank bag full of cash," Tess was saying.

"I agree," LuAnn said. "I'm just saying that even though it sounds crazy, it doesn't mean it's not true. People do strange things all the time."

"She's one of the few people who had access to the money, and one of the people who needs it the most," Tess said.

"Right," Janice said, coming up to join them. "But she's also one of the people with the most to lose. It's her mom who's gotten blamed for this. Her mom the police are interrogating and who might lose her recording contract if she's arrested." Janice sighed. "I know it looks suspicious, but I just don't see how she could be responsible."

"And I don't see how she couldn't be," Tess said. "Look, Janice, please don't take this the wrong way. But you're thinking of this like a mom, like a grandmother, not like a detective. I worry you're blinded by the fact that Brin is about to become your granddaughter and you can't see how incredibly shady this all is."

Janice shook her head. "Oh, I see it. I just don't believe it."

"I think the only way we're going to figure this out is if we find out from Zelda how much cash was in the bank bag," LuAnn said. "I think we can do that without revealing anything about what happened today with Brin."

Janice was sure she was right, but didn't think she could be the one to make the phone call. "Great. Can you call her and have that conversation? I don't trust myself."

"Of course." LuAnn nodded. "Is Ellen all settled in?"

"I think so," Janice said.

"She seemed pretty delighted to see Brin get caught today," Tess said.

"She probably thought it was nice to see someone else take the heat for a bit," LuAnn said. She slid the onions from the cutting board into an oiled pan that was heating on the stove.

"Maybe." Janice noticed a can of tomatoes and a bulb of garlic on the counter. "That smells good. What are you making?"

"The deacons at church sent around a sign-up sheet for a meal train to help Bev while she's cooped up," LuAnn said. "I called and checked the schedule, and there was no one signed up for today, so I thought I'd bring her spaghetti."

"That was really nice of you," Janice said. "I'm sure she and Thorn will appreciate that."

"Clever too." Tess winked. Janice looked between them for a moment before she understood.

"You're going to ask her about how she ended up taking over as committee chair and her accident at Margaret's, aren't you?" Janice asked.

"I figured we would do some chatting while I'm there," LuAnn said. "Just polite conversation about topics of the day and such."

"Genius," Tess said. Janice had to admit it was a clever idea and would bless Bev and Thorn in their hour of need. She wished she'd thought of it.

"In all the hubbub about Ellen stealing clothes and Brin storing money in her car, I'd almost forgotten about the idea that Margaret could be behind this."

"Hold up. Ellen stealing what now?"

Janice realized they hadn't filled LuAnn in on what they'd learned at Antoinette's Closet. She told her what Emma had told them.

"So wait. You're telling me that around the time Ellen was in Antoinette's, clothing went missing from it?" LuAnn said as she broke some hamburger meat into small bits and added it to the onions in the pan. "And this is pretty much exactly what Ellen was arrested for previously, right?"

"That's right," Janice said.

"Well, that's convenient."

"But it's not proof of anything," Tess said. "We don't know that she had anything to do with the thefts at Antoinette's. Only that she was in the store around the same time."

"Right." Janice agreed, but knew how shady it still sounded.

"So, wait. Janice, can you get my notebook?" LuAnn held up her hands, which were covered in hamburger. Janice retrieved the notebook and a pen from the coffee table and started to write. "So Ellen is still definitely a suspect. And sadly, we have to add Brin back to the list, at least until we talk to Zelda about how much cash was in the bank bag."

Janice nodded. "I'm sure we'll be able to take her off again after that."

"Right," LuAnn said. She was placating Janice, but Janice didn't care. "We crossed Jessica Landry off the list."

"I think that was the right call," Tess said. "I believed her story."

"She had the battle wounds to prove it," Janice said, clicking the pen.

"And we've still got Margaret as someone with a motive," LuAnn said, reading from the notebook. "She wanted to get back in charge of the committee."

"Hopefully we'll find out more about that from Bev tonight," Janice said. "Because of your genius plan."

"That just leaves Zelda," Tess said.

"And it wasn't her," Janice said.

"Of course not," LuAnn said. "None of us want to believe it could be her."

Janice slammed the notebook shut. "So let's just prove it's not."

CHAPTER EIGHTEEN

November 3, 1859

That night, Prudence walked the floor during the wee hours of the morning holding the infant girl. She wondered when the morning would come. Sweet Moses with his beautiful curls and chubby arms and legs lay sound asleep as he had almost since his birth. Perhaps this baby was missing her mama, or a lack of consistent care had caused her to fuss.

Either way, this night Prudence was not meant for sleep. When the morning did dawn and both babies were asleep at the same time, she made her usual trip down to the river. There she spied the sign that packages would be delivered tonight.

Her heart sank. How would she manage to get through a day without sleep only to be presented with another night of the same? She tucked the ribbon into her pocket and continued her trek to the river.

"Shame on thee," Prudence said aloud as Patience the goose looked up at her. "Thee is complaining about a little thing like sleep when there are babies without mamas and good people whose freedom is taken from them."

"Does the goose ever respond?"

Prudence jumped at the sound of the unfamiliar voice. A woman of middle years with a stern expression studied her from the path that ran alongside the river. Her clothes were that of a lady, and she wore her dark hair in the latest style. While nothing about her appeared to show wealth, there was an air of authority about her that put Prudence on notice to be concerned.

"I know who you are, Mrs. Willard."

Was she friend or foe? Prudence did not know. She could be either. But whoever she was, she had just seen Prudence take the ribbon. If she knew what that meant, all could be lost.

Chapter Nineteen

LuAnn was just tossing the noodles into the boiling water when the doorbell rang downstairs.

"I'll go see who it is," Janice volunteered, and a minute later, she opened the door to find Paul Townsend standing on the porch. He had pink cheeks and was wearing what looked like athletic pants under his coat, and he had on sneakers. He looked totally different than the put-together bank president they'd seen the day before.

"Hello, Paul. Come in."

"Thank you." He followed her inside and took his fleece cap off his head as she closed the door behind him. "Sorry for how I look. Charlotte has been checking my FitBit, so I'm walking home today to try to get my steps in."

"I'm sure the exercise is good for you," she said, trying to hold back a smile. *Especially if you're still sneaking burgers and fries*, she thought, but managed to bite her tongue.

"I know Charlotte is doing this all out of love, but it sure doesn't seem like it in the moment," he said. "Anyway, I wanted to let you know that our auditor got back to us, and it seems that everything is aboveboard. All the records checked out, and there were no irregular deposits from the things dropped in over the weekend."

"But..." Janice struggled for words. "I don't understand. What about that security camera footage?" She'd emailed the footage to Paul the day before. "It shows Zelda putting the bag in the deposit box."

"I've forwarded the footage to the police, so they have it for their investigation," Paul said. "But all it shows is Zelda going up to the deposit box and opening it. It doesn't show whether she actually put the bag in the box. You just can't see that from the camera angle, and with the distance..."

Tess and LuAnn had said the same thing, but Janice didn't buy it. "Where else would she have put it?"

"I wish I could say," Paul said. "All I can tell you for sure is that the bank bag wasn't in the deposit box when it was opened Monday morning."

Janice heard something in his words, and she felt a spark of hope. "Then someone had to have opened the box from the inside of the bank *before* Monday morning." That had to be what happened. It was the only way to explain the fact that Zelda had put the bag into the deposit box, but it had vanished before Monday. "Who had access to the box over the weekend?"

Paul sighed. "No one was in the bank after we closed Saturday until Monday morning."

"No one? What about security guards?"

"The security is monitored remotely," Paul said. "And there would have been no reason for anyone to have been in the bank over the weekend."

"No *good* reason," Janice clarified. "But that doesn't mean no one was there. Who has keys to the building?"

Paul sighed. "I do, and the managers all have them as well. But to get into any area where money is kept, an employee would need to swipe a key card. So if someone came in over the weekend and took anything from the box, there would be a record of it. And there's nothing."

Janice pondered this. Surely key card systems could be manipulated. If she was right that Zelda had deposited that money into the night deposit box, then someone inside the bank had to have taken it. There was no other explanation.

"I'm sorry I can't give you the answer you were hoping for," Paul said. "But I can assure you that we're taking this very seriously."

Janice knew they were—this whole thing wasn't helping the bank's reputation, especially once it had come out that their security cameras had been disabled—but it sure didn't feel like it.

She thanked Paul and saw him out, then she turned to head back upstairs to let Tess and LuAnn know what Paul had said. She was halfway up the stairs when the inn's phone rang. She went back to the registration desk.

"Wayfarers Inn," she said. "How can I help you?"

"Hi. This is Merri. From Olive?"

It took her a moment to catch up. "Oh! The store with the banana shirt!" They had never learned the saleswoman's name.

"Uh…sure. Anyway, when you were in here the other day, you said to call if I remembered anything about when those two women were in here Saturday."

"Right." Janice felt her heartbeat speed up. "Did you think of something?"

"It may be nothing," Merri said, "but you asked, and so, well, I thought I would just put it out there."

"Put what out there?"

"A number of items went missing from inventory Saturday evening," Merri said.

"Went missing?"

"Stolen. A few T-shirts, a purse, and a puffer jacket were stolen sometime in the late afternoon Saturday. It happened around the time your friends were here."

"Oh."

"So I thought, you know, if either of them saw anything or knew where the items might be, I would love to get them back, no questions asked."

"Oh." Janice saw what she was getting at now. "Right. Well, I can certainly try to find out if they"—she paused—"saw anything."

"Thank you," Merri said.

Janice hung up the phone and headed upstairs again.

LuAnn was just finishing packing up the spaghetti to take to the Thorntons. Janice told her and Tess about what Paul had said and about the phone call from Merri at Olive. Then she flopped down on the couch.

"Ellen could have taken the items from Olive and planned to resell them online," Tess said.

"In some ways, that makes a lot more sense than Ellen shopping there," Janice said. "I can't figure out how she could afford those prices."

"It turns out maybe she didn't need to," Tess said. "She was never planning to pay for them."

"We don't know that for sure," LuAnn said. "It's just a theory."

But Janice couldn't help but feel it was true. She set her feet up on the coffee table and let her head loll to the side.

"Janice," LuAnn said in a cheerful voice, "I could sure use your help delivering this meal to Bev." She smiled sweetly.

It was an unmistakable effort to distract Janice from the funk she'd settled into. Janice hesitated. She wasn't sure she really wanted to be distracted, and on top of that, she still had doubts that Margaret could have managed to pull off a scheme like this just to regain control of the Thanksgiving committee. But Tess pointed out that delivering a meal to someone in need was a good thing to do, whether or not she could provide a clue to the mystery. Janice had to agree.

"I'll stay here and call Jeff Jr. to make sure we're square on borrowing his truck for the Christmas parade," Tess said.

A few minutes later LuAnn and Janice were headed toward the Thornton house. Tory Thornton—Thorn, as he was called—worked as a handyman around the inn sometimes. He'd had some rough years after his second wife and young daughter were killed in an accident. But he had recently remarried his first wife, Bev, and they were very happy together, as far as Janice could tell. Thorn had gotten involved in Bev's church, and he seemed to be much better off than when they'd first met him, when he'd been sleeping on the fourth floor of what was now their inn.

LuAnn pulled up in front of the brick bungalow Thorn and Bev shared. She carried the covered dish wrapped in a towel, and Janice carried a green salad and a homemade vinaigrette. LuAnn rang the doorbell, and Thorn opened the door.

"Hello Janice, LuAnn." He gestured for them to step inside and then shut the door behind them. "Thank you so much for bringing this. Bev and I really appreciate it. I don't know what we would do without the people from the church taking care of us. Bev has been in so much pain, and I'm hopeless in the kitchen."

"We're glad to do it," LuAnn said. "People in the church are supposed to look out for each other." She set the dish down on the counter, and Janice set the salad beside it.

"Well, I'm thankful. And it doesn't hurt that the church is full of really good cooks." Thorn laughed as he lifted the lid to take a peek. "This looks delicious."

"It's nothing much," LuAnn said. "Tomatoes aren't in season, so I had to use canned. But I hope you enjoy it."

"I'm sure we will." He smiled. "Now, I'm sure you probably have to run off, but Bev would be so disappointed if you didn't at least go in and say hello. She gets lonely cooped up in the living room all day, and she really looks forward to visitors. Do you have a minute to say hello?"

"Absolutely," Janice said. "We were looking forward to talking with her."

Thorn led them through the kitchen into the living room, where Bev was lying on the couch under a blanket. She was watching a sitcom that had originally been on the air more than twenty years ago, but she used the remote control to mute it when Janice and LuAnn walked in.

"Hello," Bev called from the couch. "Welcome. Have a seat. Thank you so much for stopping in."

"Of course. How are you doing?" Janice took a seat in the armchair across from the couch, and LuAnn sat on the piano bench. Janice had been on many visits of this sort as a pastor's wife, and she easily found herself slipping back into that role.

"I've been all right," Bev said. "I've been in pain, but the doctor says things are healing up nicely, so hopefully it will only be a few more weeks of this."

"Oh, wow," Janice said. "A few more weeks?" The accident had been over two weeks ago.

"Yes, well. I'm trying to look on the bright side. At least it gets me out of cooking a turkey this year."

Janice laughed, though her mind was already working. Bev was exactly the kind of person who would be helped by the Thanksgiving Feast. And exactly the kind of person who would be hurt if the event didn't go forward as planned.

"I was so sorry to hear that you had to step down as the Thanksgiving Feast committee chair," LuAnn said, smoothly bringing the subject around to what they wanted to discuss. "That must have been a big disappointment."

"Honestly? Not so much." She looked guilty for a moment and then said, "Please don't take this the wrong way. I know you're very involved with the committee, Janice. But it was going to be a lot of work."

"What made you decide to volunteer in the first place?" Janice asked.

"Oh, I wouldn't exactly say I volunteered." Bev laughed. "More like I was *voluntold*."

"'Voluntold?' By who?"

"Thelma and Irene Bickerton," Bev said. "Those two may be old, but they're powerful. They're impossible to say no to."

"Did they say why they wanted you to volunteer for the job this year?" LuAnn asked.

"I believe it had something to do with centerpieces," Bev said.

LuAnn looked as confused as Janice felt. "Centerpieces?"

"Apparently, the Bickerton sisters got into a snit with Margaret Ashworth last year over the centerpieces at the community meal. Thelma thought they looked tacky and cheap, and said as much to Margaret."

"Oh, dear." Margaret Ashworth would not have taken that well.

"Naturally, Margaret got defensive. Donations were down, they didn't have enough of a budget, the Bickertons themselves had given less than in previous years…you can imagine how those excuses went over."

Sadly, Janice could imagine it only too well. She knew the parties involved, and they were all proud and stubborn.

"I spent the holiday with Stacy and Larry last year, but I did deliver a few meals, so I stopped by and saw the tables all laid out," Janice said. "I thought the flowers looked lovely."

"Thorn and I ate at the church, and I certainly didn't pay too much attention to the flowers. I was so grateful for the food I wouldn't have cared if there were baskets of spaghetti used as decorations," Bev said. "And I work in a floral shop."

"So Thelma and Irene wanted Margaret to step aside as chair of the committee because they didn't like the flower arrangements last year?" Janice wanted to make sure she was understanding this correctly.

"That's what I was told. I don't know. It sounds silly, doesn't it? But I suppose it probably started as a fight over flowers and escalated from there. My guess is it was really about a hundred little slights and insults that happened over the past fifty years."

Janice realized Bev was probably right. Thelma, Irene, and Margaret had all lived in this town most of their lives. There was a decent chance that the fight wasn't really about the flowers at all.

"In any case, Irene asked me to stand for chair when it was time for the committee to vote," Bev said. "I've been working at Blooms for the past six months. You know, the florist shop on Front Street?"

They both nodded. They knew the place.

"Well, I suppose they were hoping for a discount on flowers so they could, well, spruce things up a bit. I had to promise them that there would be no carnations in the centerpieces this year."

"What's wrong with carnations?" Janice asked. "I like carnations."

LuAnn met Bev's eye, like they were sharing some secret message.

"They're like the honeydew of the flower world," LuAnn said. "Filler."

"I *like* honeydew," Janice said. "So, what? Does everyone hate carnations except me?"

Bev laughed. "I don't mind them. They can be pretty. But they're on the cheaper side of things, and apparently Thelma and Irene were going for something a bit more upscale."

"Well," Janice said. "Point noted."

"If I'd known how much trouble it was going to cause and how hurt Margaret would be, I never would have said yes," Bev said. "I suppose that's part of why they asked me, because I didn't have the history, so I didn't know how much hurt I was causing and the mess I was stepping into."

"I was told there were many people who were in favor of a change of pace," Janice said. She had missed the meeting because they'd had a wedding at the inn that afternoon. It was a close vote, but in the end, Bev was the new committee chair.

"How did Margaret respond to the vote?" Janice asked.

"Oh, you know. Not well," Bev said. "She was hurt, and now that I know more of the history, I can see why. She'd run this event for so long, it can't have felt good to have someone like me come in and take over. That's why I went to the museum, actually. To apologize to Margaret."

"That's when you fell, right?" Janice asked.

"Exactly. Which just goes to show, you should never apologize." Bev laughed and then grimaced.

"Oh, dear. Is there anything we can do to help?" Janice asked.

"No. It's almost time for more pain medication, so I'll just hold on for that," Bev said.

"Can you tell us how it happened, at the museum?" LuAnn asked.

"You mean, did Margaret try to take me out so she could be chair again?" Bev shook her head. "I'm afraid it was nothing that dramatic. I came in and didn't find her right away. I was looking for her when I tripped on a step."

"So you don't think there's any way she was behind it?" Janice asked.

"It would make a much better story, wouldn't it? 'Octogenarian Museum Director Takes Out Rival over Charity Thanksgiving Meal.' But sadly, I'm afraid that's not what happened. I tripped like a dope. And Margaret couldn't have been more helpful, calling the ambulance and calling Thorn to meet me at the hospital." She adjusted her position on the couch. "Besides, if that was her plan, it didn't work out all that well for her, did it? The committee picked Zelda to be the chair, not Margaret."

Janice had been at that meeting, and she had been happy to vote for her son's girlfriend to head up the event. She had even thought that having a singer with some name recognition in charge might lead to an uptick in donations—and she had been right about that, though it hadn't exactly helped in the end. She hadn't even thought about what it must have felt like for Margaret to have to hand over control of the committee she'd chaired for so many years.

"Thank you very much for your time," LuAnn said, pushing herself up. "We appreciate your talking with us."

"Are you kidding? I appreciate your stopping by. And thank you for the food. I'll have Thorn bring the containers back in the next few days."

"Oh, don't worry about that," Janice said. "We'll be praying for your swift recovery."

As they drove back to the inn, they discussed what they had learned. "Well, at least now we're sure Margaret didn't set up Bev's injury as a way to take back control of the committee," Janice said.

"Thank goodness. That would be so diabolical." LuAnn signaled and turned right onto Fourth.

"It doesn't mean that she couldn't have taken the money to set Zelda up though," Janice said. "If she really wanted to be in charge of the committee all that badly, she could have made it happen."

"I guess…" LuAnn said slowly. "But again. What you're talking about is not only horrible—setting up a single mother to take the fall for thousands of missing dollars—it's also grand theft. We're talking the potential for serious jail time here. Would Margaret really do all that for a position as chair of a volunteer committee?"

"It does sounds kind of crazy, now that you say it like that," Janice admitted.

"There's also the problem of opportunity," LuAnn said. "Unless Margaret took the money at the meeting, which we're sure she didn't do, when would she have taken it? She didn't go into Zelda's house, and unless she broke into the bank somehow, I don't see how she could have taken it."

"That's another good point," Janice said. "All right. It was always kind of a stretch to consider Margaret anyway."

"It was," LuAnn agreed. "Logic rules her out pretty easily. I'll cross her off the list when we get home."

Janice sighed and watched the houses and trees go by outside the window.

Just as they were pulling into the driveway, LuAnn's phone rang. "Can you grab that for me?" she asked. Janice dug through her purse and found the phone and saw that it was Zelda calling.

"Hi, Zelda. This is Janice, answering LuAnn's phone. She's driving at the moment."

"Oh, hi, Janice. I was just calling LuAnn back. She'd called earlier to ask how much cash was in the bank bag I deposited on Saturday." Zelda told Janice the total, which was even larger than she'd imagined, and then told her how much of that was cash. It was more than the amount of cash that she'd found in Brin's car.

Which didn't prove Brin's innocence. She could have already spent some of the cash, possibly to pay back the school.

"Thank you," Janice said. "That's helpful to know."

"Does this mean you're getting closer to finding out what happened to the money?"

Janice could hear the hope in her voice.

"We're getting closer," Janice said. "I'll let you know if we find anything more."

"That would be great," Zelda said, and ended the call.

"It sounds like the cash in Brin's car could be the money we're looking for," LuAnn said.

Janice let out a sigh. "I suppose it could be," she said. But for Stuart's sake, everything in her hoped it wasn't.

CHAPTER TWENTY

When they got back to the inn, a pair of old friends on a girls' getaway were just coming back in from dinner. Janice and LuAnn chatted with them for a while, and then they talked to an older couple from Detroit who were planning to spend the week with their daughter and her family. They stopped in at Ellen's room to see if she needed anything, but she didn't answer the knock at the door. Either she was busy or she'd gone out, Janice figured. Together, she and LuAnn headed back upstairs and found Tess hunched over her laptop on the couch. Tom was curled up against her thigh, purring.

"Hello," Tess called, without looking up. "How did it go?"

"It was enlightening," LuAnn said. She settled down on the other side of the couch to explain what Bev had said. Janice sat down across from them. Tess nodded as LuAnn talked, but she was looking at the screen the whole time.

"What's so interesting over there?" LuAnn leaned over and glanced at Tess's computer screen. "Wait. Are you shopping?"

"Not shopping." Tess turned the screen so they could both see it. "Researching."

Janice saw that she was looking at eBay, an online auction site. "While you two were out, I called Emma over at Antoinette's Closet."

"So you are shopping," LuAnn said, smiling so Tess knew she was joking.

"I was thinking about what you said about why Ellen had been arrested," Tess said. "For stealing things and selling them online. So I had an idea. I asked Emma for specifics about the things that were stolen. Color, size, brand, etc. She couldn't tell me specifics on everything, but she described several of the scarves that were missing. And she knew the brands and sizes of the jackets and shoes. And she said there was a small stain on the sleeve of the jacket."

"So you're trying to find an online store selling them." Janice put the pieces together. "To see if Ellen is behind it."

"Exactly." Tess nodded.

"So. Did you find anything?"

"I did find a seller that recently listed two silk scarves and a jean jacket for sale, but there's not enough information listed about the jacket for me to be able to tell if there's a chance it's the same one. I emailed the seller to ask about whether there are any stains or tears. So we'll see what they come back with."

"Can you see where the seller is located?" Janice asked.

"It's listed as Ohio, but it doesn't get any more specific than that," Tess said.

"So it could be the stolen merchandise," LuAnn said. "And if so, there's a chance it's Ellen who listed it."

"Even if she is selling stolen goods online, it doesn't prove that she's behind the missing money," Janice said. "But it sure makes it easier to believe that she could be."

"I'll let you know if I hear back from the seller," Tess promised. "Now, is there any more of that spaghetti? It smells so good."

"I made a double batch so we would have some for ourselves." LuAnn pushed herself up and walked to the kitchenette, where a covered pan waited on the stove. LuAnn lit the burner beneath it.

"Have I ever mentioned how grateful I am to live with you?" Tess said.

"The feeling is mutual." LuAnn gestured toward the open laptop while Janice got up to set the table. A few minutes later, LuAnn was dishing out spaghetti onto the plates and Janice noticed that she was being unusually quiet.

Janice turned to her friend. "Is everything all right?"

"I was just thinking," LuAnn said.

"That'll get you into trouble every time," Tess joked.

LuAnn smiled and continued. "I was thinking how strange it is that two of our suspects are Christian musicians."

"Christians mess up just like everyone else," Janice said. She'd seen it so many times as a pastor's wife. People who looked like they had it all together, who looked like spiritual giants, were just as prone to misstep as anyone else. "Being a Christian doesn't mean you're immune to sin, just forgiven for it."

"I know that's true," LuAnn said. "It's just hard to think that someone whose career is dedicated to glorifying and praising God would be suspected of something like this."

"*Suspected* is the key word here," Janice insisted. "We don't know that either one of them has anything to do with taking the money."

The three women sat at the table and joined hands to say grace. Janice knew without asking that mixed in with their thanks were heartfelt prayers for guidance and wisdom as they continued to search for clues to clear their friends.

CHAPTER TWENTY-ONE

Janice woke up early Friday morning, her mind spinning. There was less than a week until Thanksgiving. Less than a week to find that money. The final planning meeting was tomorrow, and they would need to decide how to proceed then, but Janice hoped they could move forward on faith, even if they hadn't found the money yet. She lay in bed for a moment, praying for God to guide her steps and to help them find the truth. "And let Zelda and her girl be innocent, please," she added.

When Janice went downstairs, the inn was bustling with activity as customers arrived. Almost every table at the café was filled, and Taylor was already replacing the coffee urn on the counter.

"You look determined," Winnie said as Janice stepped into the kitchen.

"I am. I'm determined to solve this mystery of where the bank bag went," Janice said. "And I'm determined that the Thanksgiving Feast will go forward as planned. There are too many people who rely on this meal for it to be canceled."

Winnie chuckled as she wiped her hands on a dish towel. "I'm fully on board with that. I plan to bake plenty of pies to contribute to the cause. It doesn't matter if you find that money or not, I'm going to do everything I can to make sure no one goes without pie this Thanksgiving."

Janice laughed, and then she reached to pat Winnie's hand. "I love that idea."

Winnie laughed. "And I love pie."

Janice had a thought. "Winnie," she said, "Wayfarers can contribute the ingredients for the pies. I know Tess and LuAnn will love to be a part of your giving. Please order and use whatever you need to make the pies for the feast."

"Thank you," Winnie said. "I sure do appreciate that."

The bell rang on the inn's front door, and Janice turned to go. "I'd better see who it is. If I remember correctly, we've got a couple coming from Charleston who requested an early check-in."

"All right." Winnie rose and headed back to the stove. "Oh, and Janice," she said. "Remember, the Lord knows where that bag is. I'm still asking Him to hurry."

"Thank you." Janice grinned. "And I've been asking Him to hurry faster."

She stepped out into the hall, allowing the kitchen door to close behind her. Breakfast service was still in progress, although most of the early risers had already finished their meals and were either gone or looked as though they were about to leave.

Instead of finding guests at the front desk, Janice spied her son waiting there. "Stuart," she called out as she closed the distance between them to give him a hug. "I'm so glad to see you this morning."

"Thanks, Ma. I finished my rounds at the hospital and thought I would stop by before I go in to the office."

Janice leaned back to look up at him. Oh, how handsome he was. There was so much of his father in him, and yet she could see some of herself too.

She stepped out of his embrace but kept her hand on his arm for just a moment longer before she rested it on the desk.

"I heard you got to go out to the studio and watch Zelda cut a track." He shook his head. "I'm jealous. She won't let me watch her. Says it makes her nervous."

"Well, I'm thrilled we were allowed. She's so talented, Stuart. Her voice...is beautiful."

"I agree," he said. And then he got quiet. No doubt trying to figure out how to say what he'd come here to say, Janice guessed.

The front door opened, jangling the bells and allowing a blast of cold air to blow in. The newlyweds who had checked in yesterday hurried inside. From their attire, she assumed they had been out running. Things had certainly changed since she went on her honeymoon with Lawrence.

"Good morning," she called as they waved and then hurried over to take up spots in the café. She turned back to Stuart.

"So...I...I heard about what happened with the money under Brin's car seat yesterday," he finally stammered.

"I figured." What else would bring him here before work like this? "So Brin told her mom?"

He nodded. "Zelda thought it was odd when LuAnn called to ask how much cash had been in the bank bag, and Brin doesn't have a poker face. She confessed everything to Zelda—

about failing a class, losing the scholarship, taking the job at the bank. I know it looks bad, but Mom, she insists that this part of her story is true. That the money in her car is the money from her job. And I want you to know, she's a good kid. She wouldn't steal anything. Especially not when it's her mom who would have to take the fall. It wouldn't make sense, even if she had it in her."

"I want to believe that. And part of me does. But at the same time, she lied to me about her job. I just don't know if I can trust her."

"I'll admit that she's made some poor choices," Stuart said. "Not just with the lying, although that too. But with school and with the decision to hide the money in her car for safekeeping?" He shook his head. "That part doesn't make sense to me. But it must have made sense to her, and just because logic isn't her strong suit, it doesn't mean she's guilty."

"I hope you're right," Janice said.

"Anyway, so far the police don't seem to know about the cash from Brin's car, and we'd really like to keep it that way. It would be so easy for them to drag her into this, and for the police to try to make it seem like it was related."

"I see." This was what he had come over to ask, then. For her silence, to protect Brin. And, as a mother, Janice could completely understand why he was asking. She would want the same thing for her own child.

"I can agree to this," Janice said. "Unless the police ask me directly, I won't volunteer anything about the money that was in her car. And I'll ask LuAnn and Tess to do the same."

"Thank you." He let out a sigh.

"Unless we find out that the money we found in Brin's car really is the money from the community meal. Then all bets are off."

"That's fine. I'm not at all worried about that being the case," Stuart said. "Thank you."

The newlyweds' laughter echoed toward them. "Of course. I want nothing more than to get this all behind us so you and Zelda can get married and give me a houseful of grandchildren."

"Okay, now, a houseful is not exactly how I see it at our age," he said with a grin. "But marriage and a child or two? Definitely."

Janice patted Stuart's arm. "All right. I'm willing to compromise," she said with a wink. "But only because I love you."

But if Brin wasn't behind the stolen money, Janice wondered, who was? Janice had been thinking about what Paul said about Zelda's financial history, turning it over in her mind, trying to figure out whether there was any chance it could be true. Now she glanced over at the coffee urn. She could use a cup. "Do you want some coffee?"

"I only have a minute, but actually, that sounds like a good idea."

"Have a seat. I'll bring you one." She gestured for him to sit down at a table in the café and poured him a cup, black, just the way he liked it. She made another cup with milk and sugar and sat down across from him. She took a sip and tried to figure out how to broach the subject that had been bothering her.

"I asked Zelda about the mortgage," Stuart said, as if reading her mind.

"Oh? What did she say?"

"You were right. She did apply for one. I could have sworn she said she decided not to go that route, but I guess I got that part of the story wrong."

Got it wrong? Or was given bad information? Paul had implied that there was a reason Zelda had been turned down. A reason bigger than not having a sufficient down payment.

"How much do you know about Zelda's past?" she asked gently.

Stuart's eyes narrowed. "I'm not sure what you're getting at."

"Has anything like this ever happened before for her?"

"Anything like what? Being on the wrong end of a bank error?"

"Like having a large amount of money vanish in her care."

"What? No. Why would you even ask that?"

Janice debated whether to tell him her reason. Ultimately, she decided he should know. "During the course of our investigation, one of the people we questioned implied there were some red flags in her financial history."

"I'm sure she would have told me if anything like this had happened before."

Janice nodded. "I believe you. I just need to be able to refute it." What else could she say?

And then a moment later she added, "Do you know how she decided to move back to Marietta?"

"I've told you all this before, Ma."

"Humor me."

He took a sip of his coffee and then said, "She lived in Nashville. She was working for a short time as a demo singer. It was a gig her agent got for her while he was shopping her for a recording deal. You met Clive at the studio, right?"

"We did," Janice said. "He seems like a very nice man."

Stuart shrugged. "I suppose. I'm not sure what I think of him right now. I think he should be fighting harder for her. The record label is threatening to pull the contract if she gets arrested or any more bad press, and I think he needs to be pushing back harder."

"How can she control what the press writes?"

"She can't. But it damages her 'brand,' I guess."

Janice wasn't sure what to think, so she gestured for Stuart to go on.

"She loved the work she was doing in Nashville, and her career was advancing, but she moved back here to be closer to her family. Plus, the cost of living in Nashville has gotten to be sky-high the past few years. And with Brin starting college, tuition was cheaper, and she could record from the studio here, so it just made sense."

"I'm sure the fact that her hunky high school sweetheart was here had something to do with it too," Janice added.

"I like to think that I might have had a little something to do with it," Stuart said. "Though we'd been apart for so long, and with Brin and everything, it wasn't a forgone conclusion that we would end up together."

"But I'm so glad you did."

"That's why we need to put this whole thing behind us," Stuart said. "So I can propose."

Janice nodded, but she was thinking through what Stuart had said.

"Stuart," Janice said slowly, "is there any benefit to Zelda's agent if the contract is canceled?"

"I can't imagine there would be," he said. "He only gets paid if Zelda makes money. She certainly can't make money without a recording contract."

"That's true. And why wouldn't he want to make money?"

"Your guess is as good as mine." Stuart drained the rest of his coffee and stood. "I'm sorry, Ma. I need to go."

"Thanks for stopping by," Janice said. "I'll keep trying to get to the bottom of this."

"I know you will." He leaned in and gave her a hug then headed for the door.

Janice sat still, thinking about Clive. There didn't seem to be any reason for him to take the money, not if the blame was likely to land on his biggest client. And how would he have taken it anyway? Zelda said she had a phone call from him Saturday, but he couldn't have taken the money through the phone. And yet, there was something nagging at her. Something that told her to look into Clive a bit more deeply. Through the course of solving so many mysteries, Janice had learned to listen to that voice.

"Earth to Janice."

Janice looked up and found Tess standing in front of her.

"Oh. Sorry. I guess I zoned out."

"I would say so." Tess sat down across from her. "What's up?"

"Probably nothing," Janice said.

"Try me."

"All right." Janice recapped her conversation with Stuart and explained that she thought she should dig into Clive's background.

"Clive? The guy who looks like Mr. Rogers?"

"I know. It's hard to imagine him doing anything shady, right? But I don't know. Something tells me he's worth looking into."

"All right then," Tess said. "There's no time like the present. Come on into the office and let's see what we can find out about Clive Clinton."

They walked into the office, and Janice sat down at the computer with Tess in the chair next to her. It took less than ten minutes to find out something very interesting about Mr. Clinton. He had tried to file for bankruptcy, but he was denied.

"What does that mean?" Janice asked.

Tess clicked a few more keys and gave Janice a triumphant look. "It looks like someone files for bankruptcy, but they don't end up qualifying, so the judge throws it out." Her eyes scanned the screen, and then she looked back up at Janice. "This says it's rare, but it does happen."

"What would cause it?"

"This website lists several reasons, including the person destroying financial books or assets, hiding assets, or hiding a previous bankruptcy when filing again."

"So it's plausible that Clive did something shady with his books or lied to the court about assets," Janice said.

"Or it was discovered that he had already filed bankruptcy and didn't cop to it."

"It's possible."

Tess was still trying to read the website. "I don't understand a word of this legalese. It would take a lawyer to decipher it."

"We do know a lawyer or two," Janice said.

"But we don't have anything specific to this case, so what would a lawyer be able to tell us?" Tess argued.

"Who needs a lawyer?" LuAnn asked, poking her head into the office.

"No one yet," Tess said. "But we've just discovered someone near and dear to Zelda who tried to file for bankruptcy and failed. Remember meeting her agent, Clive Clinton?"

LuAnn's eyes widened, and she lifted up both palms. "Don't say another word. I'm going to get my notebook."

"Just because he filed for bankruptcy a few years ago doesn't mean he has anything to do with the stolen money," Janice said.

"That's true. Just like Ellen being convicted of grand theft doesn't make her guilty of stealing the money," Tess said. "But it does make you want to find out more, doesn't it?"

Janice nodded. Her intuition was telling her there was something here, but she couldn't make sense of it. "But why would he settle for a bank bag with a decent but limited amount of money when he could get a percentage of what Zelda makes as long as her records are for sale? You heard how beautiful her voice is. Surely he can see that she'll be a star someday?"

"The key is the word 'someday.'" Tess shrugged. "What if someday isn't soon enough? Maybe he's desperate for money now."

"Is that talking I hear?" LuAnn called from the hall just before she appeared in the doorway with her notebook and pen. "I told you to wait for me."

Tess shrugged. "Get comfortable. You've got some writing to do."

LuAnn smiled as she slid into the chair beside Janice. "Okay, from the top."

Janice and Tess took turns filling her in on what they had discovered so far, first from Stuart and then from Tess's internet search. Finally, Tess sat back in her chair. "So, what do you think?" she asked LuAnn.

LuAnn paused, and she looked at Janice. "He has motive because he needs immediate cash maybe. At least we know he needed it recently. But what about opportunity?"

"And remember," Janice added, "Zelda said she doesn't get paid until the record is released, and she goes on tour. So presumably Clive doesn't either. Which means if he needs cash now, he can't wait for the record to come out."

"But how would he have gotten the money?" LuAnn asked.

"Well," Tess said slowly, "there's one person who knows both Clive and Zelda and who had access to the money before it was deposited."

LuAnn squinted. "Ellen Randall," she said.

"Bingo!" Tess leaned forward. "We already said Ellen has both proximity and motive. She is Clive's client too. That's why she was staying with Zelda. What if she knew Clive's issue with money and provided him with an answer to his troubles?"

"I see your point," LuAnn said. "But if Ellen has her own money problems, why help Clive with his?"

"To become a star," Tess said. "Clive apparently believes in her, or he wouldn't go to such extraordinary lengths to make sure she stays on the right path until she can go out on tour. He chose her as his next star, gave her the opportunity to record music, and put her in Zelda's home. Of course she would feel an obligation to help."

"I think you may be onto something," Janice said.

"That's all very interesting."

Janice whirled to see Ellen standing in the doorway.

"But you're way off base."

CHAPTER TWENTY-TWO

November 3, 1859

"You have a child," the woman said to Prudence. Prudence knew better than to give anything away.

"Moses, my son," she said.

The woman closed the distance between them, her expression now softening. "No, Mrs. Willard. You have another child."

Prudence froze. Again she said nothing rather than offer the wrong response.

"I'm terribly sorry. You do not know who I am, do you?"

"I do not," she said.

"Forgive me. I am Tabitha Sterling. Catherine Fay sent me. She has run afoul of the townspeople upon occasion, though I assure you she is a good Christian woman who wants only to see to the welfare of the youngest members of society."

"Tabitha," Prudence said on an exhale of breath. "What does thee want with me?"

A breeze rustled the tree limbs overhead, and the sound of birdsong echoed through the thicket. Prudence felt a trickle of sweat tracing a path down her spine.

"Yes, I'm sure you're wondering why I've come to see you, and more important why I have presented myself in such a covert manner rather than paying you a visit at your home."

"Indeed I had wondered," Prudence said.

"I have come to ask a favor."

It was not at all what she expected the woman to say. Rather than respond, she kept her silence.

"You are reluctant."

"Tabitha, thee has not yet asked the favor, so I cannot respond."

The woman smiled. "Yes, of course. I'm getting ahead of myself. We have received…inquiries. I believe the man who asked Miss Fay about the child may have considered her to be…property." Tabitha glanced across the river at the Virginia shore and then back at Prudence.

He was a slave owner then, come to demand what he thought of as something he owned. Judging by the child's coloring, there was a fair chance he or someone from his household was also the child's father, Prudence thought.

"Miss Fay is seeking a placement for the girl farther north. I do not think she will be safe in this area for long. For now, the man does not know where the child is. I ask only that you continue to keep the child safe for a few days longer. Give her to no one unless they come to you with a letter of introduction from me."

Prudence felt her stomach churn. She wanted to hold on to the child forever.

"Tabitha," she said slowly, "I will not expose this child to danger."

Tabitha looked past her toward the place where Prudence had plucked the ribbon from the tree. Then she slowly returned her attention to Prudence.

"You already do, Mrs. Willard."

So she knew. Still Prudence would not let Tabitha know she was correct.

Instead she asked, "What of the girl's mother?"

"I do not know for certain. But because I know of your help to our friends who travel this way…" She pointed to where the ribbon poked out of Prudence's pocket. Prudence tucked it back in quickly. "A subject I myself am also versed in, I will tell you what I guess." She paused and took in a deep breath. "I believe the child's mother saw her coloring and hoped she could have a better life. She left her where she would be found by someone likely to be sympathetic to the cause."

Prudence watched her, weighing her words. The child's mother was enslaved, she seemed to think. And seeing her child's light skin, hoped someone would find her and allow her to live as free.

It was an explanation that made sense, given the inquiries Catherine had received. And it was truly the only explanation that made sense in Prudence's heart. A mother did not abandon her child. She did not leave her infant on the ground in November, hoping a kind stranger would come along and find her, unless she had a very good reason. And freedom—the hope that because of the color of her skin, this child might live free—was one of the very few things Prudence could think of that would be worth it. No mother abandoned her baby unless she sincerely believed her sacrifice could lead to another, better life for her child. Even still, Prudence was not sure she would have had the courage. What a brave, selfless woman this child's mother must be.

Prudence believed it. And she knew the danger this knowledge placed them all in.

But she also recognized that this was exactly the situation she'd been in herself before Anna Barton took her in. And she knew that she and Jason could raise the child free.

"I will keep the child safe," she promised.

Chapter Twenty-Three

"Ellen," Tess stammered. "We...we weren't expecting you. Please come in."

Janice wanted to kick herself. What were they thinking, talking openly about Ellen like that, when she was staying in the inn and could easily overhear...and obviously had.

"Apparently." She crossed her arms over her chest.

"Come in." LuAnn hopped to her feet. "I'm sorry. We were...we were just..."

"We were wrong to be talking about you," Janice said. "And I'm sorry."

The apology seemed to take some of the wind out of Ellen's sails.

"We would love to hear the real story," Tess said. "Will you tell us?"

"Please, take my chair," LuAnn said. "I'll get a stool from the kitchen."

Ellen settled onto the chair LuAnn vacated, and a moment later LuAnn returned carrying a stool. She placed it in the doorway then picked up her pen and notebook. Once she was settled, Ellen spoke.

"And as I already said, you're wrong about Clive."

"How so?" Tess said.

"You got some of it right. He did make it possible to record my songs and to sing with Zelda. And he's determined to keep me on the right path. All of that's true. And he doesn't get paid until we tour and make some money. Then he gets a percentage. I'm still learning all of this, but there are a lot of expenses at the beginning when the album is being recorded, and the tour is being planned."

"Yes, Zelda mentioned that," Janice said. "Are you responsible for paying some of those expenses?"

"Clive is covering my share for now, but I'll have to pay him back out of my earnings eventually."

Which meant that if Clive was short on funds he would need the money now to keep the recording and tour on track.

Ellen shifted positions but kept her attention on Tess. "All that stuff about him having a reason to want to steal the cash out of that bag is way off."

"Why do you think that?"

"Because I know him." She leaned forward and rested her palms on her knees. For a moment, Janice thought she might stand and leave them without an answer. Then she smiled.

"You don't know me, but I'm pretty sure that Zelda filled you in on the basics of my background. I wasn't exactly raised by model parents. But Clive, he saw something in me. He got me out of that environment and has tried to make sure I don't go back." She paused. "I'm not the first he's done that for. There are lots of us. The problem with Clive is he's a softy. He'll fall for any sob story, and some of us have told some big ones."

"What do you mean?" LuAnn asked.

"What would you say if you were trying to get money out of someone?" Ellen asked.

When none of the women said anything, she answered her own question. "You would make up stuff like needing money for medical treatment for a sick grandma or having to sell your guitar because you're late on the rent. I think he knows when people are lying, but that's Clive. If you ask, he says yes."

"So a nice man, but not so great a businessman?" Tess offered.

"He just genuinely cares for the people he works with. And most times he's got the money to give, so it's been fine. But not always." She shrugged again.

"That's commendable," Janice said.

"Zelda would think so. She's one of them."

Janice frowned. Was that…could that have anything to do with the red flags in Zelda's credit history? Had Clive tried to help Zelda at some point?

Ellen swiveled to face Janice. "I heard you ladies talking about Clive's bankruptcy. I didn't know about that, but that must have been right after Janelle Mizuno walked away and refused to pay him his share of her earnings."

"Who?"

"You haven't heard of her?"

"No." All three of them shook their heads.

"She's another one of his clients. Or was, I should say. She had a big tour but wasn't happy with the quality of the hotels she was booked in and some other nonsense. Also, there was some argument about royalties. I don't really know the whole story, just that she left, and there was some legal fight about how she refused to pay Clive the money she owed him. I suppose he'd been counting on that to pay off expenses and finance other artists' albums."

"That sounds terrible."

"It wasn't a good scene, from what I understand. But anyway, he must have been in a bad way to file for bankruptcy."

"He tried, but he didn't succeed," Tess said. "Which means that he must have lied about something, or hidden assets, or had a previous bankruptcy or something."

"Well, I don't know about any of that. But I did hear him and Zelda talking the other day at the studio. He was saying he wouldn't be able to cover many of the upfront costs of the tour because of his financial situation." She glanced over at Janice. "I pay attention. People think I'm not listening, but I am."

"How did Zelda respond to that news?" LuAnn asked.

"She was worried because she doesn't have money saved to cover the costs herself," Ellen said. "Which, yeah, I know, looks bad. But after what happened last time, I know she would want to do everything aboveboard."

"What do you mean, 'what happened last time'?" Janice asked.

"Oh, you didn't hear about this? Before Clive, Zelda was working with another manger. A real bad guy, from what I understand. The story is that the band she was singing with was going to have to cancel their tour because there wasn't enough money, and Zelda volunteered to put a big chunk of it on her credit card because he promised she'd get paid back soon. Well, naturally, that didn't happen, and he ran off with the money. Tanked her credit, and she was out thousands of dollars. That's the story that went around, anyway. I don't know how much of it is true, of course, and I haven't had the guts to ask her."

"That's terrible," LuAnn said. Janice agreed. How could someone treat sweet Zelda like that? She didn't want to believe it, but it did line up with what Paul Townsend had hinted about a mortgage. She would have had a hard time getting a mortgage if her credit had been ruined by an unscrupulous manager.

"There was a rumor that that's why she left Nashville, but I don't think it's true. I believe she really did want to move home," Ellen said. "And of course she signed on with Clive, and he's one of the good guys. So I know he didn't take it. And I saw Zelda deposit the money, so I know she didn't take it."

Janice pursed her lips. She wanted to believe Ellen.

"Besides. I didn't take the money out of Zelda's purse and pass it to him. So how would he have gotten it? Unless you want to suggest that Zelda gave it to him herself?"

"No, that doesn't make sense," LuAnn said.

Actually, it was plausible, Janice thought. If Zelda had taken the money out of the bank bag and then deposited it empty, Ellen would never have known the money was gone. And then Zelda could have given it to Clive to cover tour expenses.

But why would she have done that when she was certain to be the one to get blamed? And with the morality clause in her contract, they all stood to lose if the theft got pinned on Zelda. No, it just didn't make sense.

"I suppose we should take Clive Clinton off the list," Janice said.

"I'll move him down," LuAnn said. "But not off altogether."

Ellen rose. "Suit yourselves. But you'll be telling me I was right soon enough."

"I hope so," Janice said. "Your agent seems like a very nice man. I want to believe that he isn't involved in any way."

"And I'm not involved either," Ellen said with a shrug of her shoulder. "I know how it looks. I've got motive and opportunity. But I'm telling the truth. If I was going to steal something, I certainly wouldn't want to get Zelda in trouble in the process. I owe her too much to treat her like that."

Janice reached over to pat Ellen's arm.

Ellen gave her what appeared to be a genuinely warm look. Then she smiled. "Thank you, Janice." She paused. "I should go. I've got a rehearsal in half an hour, and I'm working hard not to be late."

"Thank you for talking to us," Janice said. And then, after Ellen was out of earshot, she added, "I believe Ellen, at least about Clive."

"So do I," LuAnn agreed.

Tess seemed to be considering the statement. Then, finally, she nodded. "I think she's telling us what she knows. Whether it's *all* she knows is another question."

"Do you think she's hiding something?" LuAnn asked.

Tess tilted her head. "I don't know. There's just something about how she phrased her responses that struck me as not being fully forthcoming."

"And she did answer our questions with questions a few times," Janice added. "Lawrence always said that's a sure sign there's more to what a person is saying than what they're actually telling you."

"I agree with Lawrence," Tess said.

"Me too," LuAnn said. "Her explanation of what happened with the bankruptcy, the other artist who walked away, all of that makes sense."

"He did seem very kind when I met him," Janice said. "And Zelda has spoken highly of him to me in the past." She shrugged. "It all adds up when you look at everything Ellen told us."

They were all quiet for a moment, and then Janice spoke. "So why don't I believe her?"

Neither Tess nor LuAnn had an answer.

"I hate to bring this up now," LuAnn said. "Well, actually, I hate to bring this up at any point. But did you guys see the newspaper today?"

"No." Janice let out a sigh. "Do I want to?"

"Probably not," LuAnn said. "But if you change your mind, it's on the check-in desk."

"I'll go get it," Tess said, pushing herself up. Janice saw her check to make sure everything in the café was running smoothly, and then she grabbed the newspaper and returned to the office.

Local Christian Singer Lead Suspect in Missing Charity Cash, the headline read.

"I don't even want to see the rest of it," Janice said. She stood and turned around. "I'll go help Taylor with breakfast. At least that will distract me from all this for a while."

After breakfast had been cleaned up and the smell of roasting vegetables was filling the air—surely that meant Winnie was making her carrot ginger soup for the lunch crowd—Janice headed up to the fourth floor. She had an idea. She wasn't at all sure it would get her any closer to finding answers, but she needed to see for herself.

"I'm going to go to the bank," she said. LuAnn looked up from the couch where she was reading a book, both animals curled up next to her. Tess was hunched over her laptop again. "Does anyone want to come with me?"

"I'm deep in eBay investigation," Tess said. "So I'll pass."

"I'll come," LuAnn said. She placed the bookmark in her book and gently moved Tom off her lap. The cat protested with a yowl, but he settled down in the spot she had just vacated. "Let me get my purse."

A few minutes later they were in Janice's car. "So what are we doing at the bank? Are you going to go in there, guns blazing, and demand answers?"

"I don't think going inside a bank brandishing a gun sounds like a very good idea," Janice said. "Sadly, I'm hoping to do something much more sedate. I want to see if someone will show me the inside of the overnight deposit box."

"That is less fun," LuAnn said. "Why?"

"I just want to understand what happened. I want to know what happens once a night deposit goes into the building."

"Paul said that he completely trusts the woman who emptied it," LuAnn said. "And the auditor said there was nothing irregular with the deposits."

"And I'm sure they're both right," Janice said. "I just want to see it for myself."

"I'm game," LuAnn said. "We'll see if they're willing to show us."

When they arrived at the bank they saw a maintenance worker scrubbing graffiti off an outside wall. Paul explained that as soon as they'd gotten the outside security cameras fixed, the hooligans had come back with another prank, this time spray-painting pigs on the side of the historic building.

"Pigs?" Janice asked.

"Capitalist pigs, I assume," Paul said with a shrug. "In any case, it'll be gone soon."

They explained why they were there, and Paul was hesitant to let them see the inner workings of the bank deposit system, but all it took was a little persuasion for him to relent. He introduced them to Tara, a woman in her fifties with a no-nonsense suit and pumps, and asked her to show them how she had emptied the night deposit box Monday morning.

She led them through a door that let them into the back office, and then they walked behind the tellers toward the wall where the ATM and deposit boxes were. The area was walled off from the main area occupied by the tellers. "You need to swipe a key card to get access to this area," Tara said, sliding a plastic card through a slot attached to the door handle. She opened the door and led them inside the small space. "So there would be a record of anyone who came in here. And I'm the only one who came in on Monday. The security cameras in here back that up." She pointed to the cameras on the ceiling.

"That's the back of the ATM?" LuAnn pointed to a silver metal cabinet with a keypad.

"That's right." Tara nodded. "Only a handful of us know the code to get it open. We empty it every morning and every night and restock the cash."

"And is that the night deposit box?" Janice pointed to another, smaller metal box higher on the wall. This one had a keyhole in the silver door.

"That's right." Tara slid a plastic bracelet off her wrist and used the attached key to unlock the box. She had to pull hard, but she managed to open the door, and they saw that it was really just a metal box attached to the wall. "I opened this first thing Monday morning and emptied it."

"And then what did you do with the deposits?" LuAnn asked.

"I brought everything to the counter and ran the cash through the counting machine and the checks through the scanners and then entered the totals into the proper accounts," Tara said.

Janice bent down and looked inside the night deposit box. All she could see was the underside of the metal lid. It was bowed, with the middle dipping down. She kept looking around, hoping for more, for any sort of clue about where that money might have gone, but she couldn't find anything.

LuAnn was looking at Janice, waiting to see if she was satisfied. Janice supposed she had to be. She didn't know what she'd been hoping to find, but there was nothing irregular here as far as she could see.

"Thank you for showing us," Janice said as Tara closed the deposit box back up. She struggled with closing it, but finally it clicked shut.

"Does it always do that?" LuAnn asked.

"It has since those kids threw that firecracker in it," Tara said. "I keep trying to convince Paul we should get a new one, but he doesn't want to spend the money since this one works fine. You just have to jiggle it a little."

On the drive back to the inn, LuAnn was quiet.

"What's going through your head?" Janice asked.

"I was wondering if we have to just accept that the money is gone for good."

"It's not like you to give up."

"I can't figure it out. The money wasn't taken before the bank bag was deposited. But it wasn't taken after it was deposited either. So where did it go? It's like it vanished into thin air," LuAnn said.

"It didn't vanish," Janice said. "It's out there somewhere."

"That may be true," LuAnn said. "But I'm starting to wonder if it would make more sense to stop worrying about what happened to it and just accept the fact that it's gone. Then we can focus on making sure we collect enough money to replace it so the feast can still go on."

Janice nodded, but she didn't say anything the whole way home. If it wasn't for the fact that Stuart was about to propose to Zelda, she would have agreed. But even though she couldn't give up, not when Stuart's bride was on the line, it really was starting to feel hopeless.

CHAPTER TWENTY-FOUR

When they got home, Tess was helping Robin serve lunch in the café, but something had happened. Janice could see it on her face.

"What's going on?"

"Hang on." Tess was carrying a tray of soup bowls, and she delivered them to a couple in the corner before she waved to let Robin know she was stepping out for a bit. She met LuAnn and Janice in the office. Tess looked around carefully, and then she whispered, "It's not her."

"What?" LuAnn said in a normal tone of voice.

"Shh!" Tess shushed her with her hands. "I don't want her to overhear again."

"Ellen?" Janice whispered.

Tess nodded. "The eBay seller I was following? The one I thought might be Ellen? It's not her."

"How do you know?" Janice asked.

"Because I tracked her down," Tess said.

"That sounds more than slightly ominous," LuAnn said.

"I tracked her down online, I mean. Well, first I noticed that even though some of the items she was selling seemed to match up with the things that were taken from Olive and Antoinette's, there were also a few things that didn't match.

Clothes from major chain stores that we don't have in Marietta mostly. So I started poking around. I compared her username to other places that name was used online and was able to track down a profile for her there."

"Please tell me you didn't do anything illegal," Janice said.

"Of course not," Tess said. "But in any case, I figured out who it was. It's a mom in Cleveland who resells things she finds at local thrift stores. She has three kids, a Maltipoo, and a fondness for pumpkin spice lattes."

"That's random," LuAnn said.

"Agreed," Janice said. "But it's definitely not Ellen."

"That doesn't mean Ellen isn't fencing stolen goods online. Just that I didn't find any record of it," Tess said.

"I guess that's good, right?" LuAnn asked.

"I hope so." Tess shook her head. "I don't even know anymore."

Janice wasn't sure she knew either.

⁓❦⁓

Later that afternoon, Janice was cleaning Woodbine and Roses after the guests had checked out when LuAnn came into the room.

"Janice? You should come downstairs." LuAnn was out of breath like she'd been running.

Janice dropped the disinfectant wipe she'd been using. "Why? What's wrong?"

"Stuart is here. He's...just hurry."

Stuart was in his late thirties, but Janice's heart would never stop dropping into her stomach when she heard that something was wrong with him. She brushed past LuAnn and ran down the two flights of stairs and found Stuart in the lobby. He was pacing between the check-in desk and the staircase, hands behind his back and thunder in his eyes.

"Stuart. What's wrong?" She ran to him and put her hand on his arm, stopping him. "Why aren't you at work?"

"She broke up with me."

"What?"

Zelda? Sweet, loving Zelda? Broke up with Stuart?

Janice was stunned. "When? Why?"

She'd broken up with *him*? She was the one accused of stealing thousands of dollars. He was trying to help her. How dare Zelda break up with him?

"She found out today that her record label was dropping her. Apparently the bad press got to be too much, and it triggered the morals clause in her contract."

"So what does that mean?"

"It means the album is off, the tour is off, the money they invested is gone with no hope of earning it back."

"But she didn't take the money."

"You know that, and I know that, but the police aren't sure, and the press certainly isn't giving her the benefit of the doubt on this."

"Oh, Stuart. I'm so sorry." Janice tried to wrap her head around this news. "But what does any of that have to do with you?"

"Nothing, as far as I'm concerned. But Zelda disagrees. She says she can't be with me now, she can't ruin my reputation, she doesn't deserve me. All kinds of nonsense."

"But you have to tell her that's ridiculous. Tell her you don't care about any of that. That you want to be with her anyway."

"I did. Repeatedly. I told her I would stand by her, no matter what. I told her I'd loved her since we were seventeen, and I'd always love her. I told her I believed in her. None of it mattered. She said she couldn't be in a relationship with me right now, and that that was the end of it."

"Oh, Stuart."

They stood still for a moment. And then he reached into his pocket and pulled out the velvet pouch she'd handed him just a few days ago.

"I came to give this back to you. It looks like I won't be needing it after all."

CHAPTER TWENTY-FIVE

November 4, 1859

Prudence made her delivery that night, meeting a woman at the edge of the thick wood. She escorted her to the inn, where Mr. Siloam would give her a bed and food to sustain her for the rest of her journey to freedom. By the time she returned home, the sun's rays were starting to brighten the horizon, and Prudence was bone-tired. But something was wrong. She saw that as soon as she stepped inside the house.

"Jason?" He should be here, but there were no candles lit, no fire in the hearth. When there was no answer, she called out again. "Jason?"

Again, no response. No sound at all, even though her shouts should have woken at least one of the babies. Prudence flew into the bedroom, but the bed was empty, and so was the crib.

"Jason!" she shouted. "Moses!"

She ran from room to room, looking for any sign of them. But the cabin was empty.

Prudence wanted to believe there was a reason for their absence. A good reason for them all to be gone. But she was exhausted, and she could not think of any good reason that Jason would have taken the children without leaving her notice.

Please, Lord, she prayed. *Please keep them safe.*

Was this it, then? Had her actions finally brought punishment on the people she loved most?

Prudence began to weep. Great, heaving sobs poured out of her, and she felt herself losing strength to stand.

But somewhere in the middle of all the emotions flooding her, she heard something. A noise.

She quieted, listening, and the sound came again. Footsteps on the porch.

Silently, carefully, she crept to the front window. A man holding a baby stood on the doorstep. Jason. Holding one baby. One.

"Pru?" Jason called softly.

Prudence flew to the door and opened it, reaching out her arms to take the sleeping Moses. Jason fell into a chair at the table, his clothes and boots caked with mud.

After laying Moses in his crib, Prudence returned to the kitchen. She was weak with relief, but also trembling in fear. She shook Jason's arm. "Jason, what has thee done? Where is the baby?"

He looked up at her, surprise overriding the exhaustion on his face. "I took her to Catherine, of course. This is not the place for her."

"Thee doesn't know that, Jason!" Prudence whirled to face him, anguished disappointment coursing through her. "Thee doesn't know what that woman will do with her."

"Prudence." Jason stood. "Remember, I warned thee not to get attached to the little one. She is not ours to keep."

Prudence turned from him, and a sob welled up in her throat. Somehow the years fell away, and the pain of losing their precious newborn daughter slammed into her heart as if she were once again looking into those perfect yet lifeless eyes. Words poured out of her—ugly words she was power-less to stop. Bitter words, accusing words, spewed at both Jason and God until she sank to the floor, overcome with grief.

CHAPTER TWENTY-SIX

Janice couldn't fall asleep Friday night. She couldn't stop thinking about the look on Stuart's face when he'd handed her the ring. Defeated. Broken.

She lay in bed and prayed for him, for the whole horrible messy situation, but the peace that prayer usually brought her remained elusive. Finally, Janice climbed out of bed and headed into the kitchenette. She would warm up some milk and see if that helped. She opened the door of the small refrigerator, but the milk carton was almost empty. Janice went back to her room, slipped on her robe, and padded downstairs. She'd get some from the main kitchen.

But when she got down to the café, the light was on, and Ellen was sitting at one of the tables. She looked up, and her mouth dropped open.

"I'm sorry, I hope I didn't wake you. I didn't know if it was okay to come down here, but I can go back up to my room if you want." Ellen wore gray sweatpants and a thin white T-shirt and cradled a mug between her hands.

"It's okay," Janice said. "You just surprised me is all. I didn't expect anyone to be down here."

"You said I should make myself at home, so I hoped you wouldn't mind." She gestured to the mug. "I couldn't sleep, and my grandma used to give me warm milk whenever I had a hard time sleeping."

"It's quite all right," Janice said. "I actually came down for the same reason."

A few minutes later, Janice came out of the kitchen with a mug of warm milk. She had planned to take the milk back up to the fourth floor, but Ellen looked so small and lonely sitting alone in the café. "Mind if I join you?" Janice asked.

"Please."

Janice pulled out the chair across from Ellen and sat down. The lights in the lobby were off, and Ellen looked younger and softer in the café's warm glow.

"I heard about Zelda and your son. I'm really sorry about that."

Janice felt tears come to her eyes. "It's really strange. I don't quite understand it. But I suppose it's not my decision."

"Nope." Ellen shook her head. "Sometimes the things that affect our lives the most are things we don't have a say over."

Janice stared at her. It was a strangely philosophical comment for midnight. "What do you mean?"

"Oh, I don't know. Maybe I'm being silly. But I was just sitting here thinking about my grandma. Today was her birthday. She would have been seventy-five."

Would have been. "She passed away?"

"A little over two years ago." She took a sip of her milk. "She raised me for the most part. But I didn't really appreciate how big a deal that was until after she was gone. I was just thinking, for like the millionth time, that I wish I'd shown her how much I appreciated it while she was alive."

"I'm sure she knew," Janice said. "I bet she wouldn't have minded hearing it, but I bet she knew. Grandmas usually do."

"You have grandkids?" Ellen asked.

"A little boy. Larry. He's six. Stuart's sister Stacy is his mom."

"That's nice." Ellen took another sip.

"Stacy is a single mom, so I help her out as much as I can," Janice said.

"Oh yeah?"

"It's not an ideal situation, but they're doing great."

"That's kind of how it started with me. My mom got pregnant really young, and my father was out of the picture by the time I was born. My grandma helped out for a while. And then my mom got married to this guy who was, well, let's just say he wasn't such a great guy. I started staying with my grandma more and more. By the time Mom finally left him, she had two more kids and a police record."

"I'm sorry," Janice said.

"It is what it is, I guess." She shrugged. "And in some ways, I was the lucky one. My little brothers still lived with her through the worst of it, and at least I had some distance. When she went into rehab, my grandma took us all in, but by that point, they'd already been through so much."

"That's awful."

"It was all right at Grandma's. She didn't have much, and we were always struggling to make ends meet, but we were safe there. And she took us to church. Another thing I didn't appreciate until it was too late to thank her."

"I'm sure she was glad to do it. A spiritual legacy is one of the most important things we can leave to our children."

"Yeah. But she didn't live long enough to see how Jesus turned my life around."

"Oh?" Janice took a sip of the warm milk and let the silence stretch out, hoping Ellen would fill it. After a moment, she did.

"I bet you heard why Clive wanted Zelda to keep an eye on me."

"I only heard that you had a troubled past. No one gave any other specifics."

The internet had offered some insights, but she didn't need to admit that now.

"I got into some trouble with shoplifting," Ellen said. "And reselling the stolen goods online."

"Ah."

"It was only because we needed the money so badly. My little brothers were hungry all the time, and Grandma had a hard time keeping up with all the bills. She didn't exactly plan to be raising three kids on her tiny pension, so it was tight. I was in this band, and I thought maybe I could make some money that way, but it turns out there wasn't a big market for thrasher music in rural Missouri."

"Go figure."

"I found that selling stolen goods paid a lot better. Enough for new clothes even. But then I got caught. And then it was bad. Lawyer fees, all that stuff, and we definitely couldn't afford it. We took a plea bargain so I could stay out of prison and finish high school, but it was hard on Grandma. She died less than a year later."

"I'm so sorry."

Again, Ellen shrugged. "I wish I could go back and redo it. But I can't, so I just have to keep moving forward."

Janice was surprised by the wisdom in those words. She knew people her own age who had trouble with that concept.

"Anyway, it wasn't until after she died that I started really thinking about all the things people talked about at her funeral. Having hope, and what faith really means, and all that. So I finally started reading my Bible, and I started to understand it in a way I never had before. That's when it became real for me. And so that's when I started singing about my faith instead of, well, whatever I was angry about at the time, and that's when things really started to take off my with music."

"That's so good to hear."

"I mean, I still don't make much at all. I think Clive really thinks I have a future in music. He's also really worried about me falling into my old ways, which is why he set me up with Zelda, so she could keep an eye on me." She chuckled. "It's kind of ironic, isn't it? That he gets me to live with her so I don't start stealing again, and then she gets blamed for stealing that money?"

Janice didn't know if it was ironic or just sad, but she nodded.

"Anyway, that's why I reacted so badly when people kept thinking I'd taken the money. Because this time I really didn't, but no one seemed to believe me. Not even Zelda. Not even you."

Janice wanted to argue, but she couldn't find the words.

"It's okay. I know you thought I took it. Maybe you still do. But I know I had nothing to do with it, and God does too. And when that money is eventually found, everyone else will know it."

Janice didn't know what it was—maybe it was the vulnerability in Ellen's voice. Maybe it was just the quiet café, or the simplicity of the soothing warm milk.

But for some reason, Janice believed her.

CHAPTER TWENTY-SEVEN

Janice attempted to concentrate on her work Saturday morning, but she found herself walking into rooms and forgetting why she was there. She was just so nervous about what was going to happen at the meeting that afternoon. The committee had to decide whether to move forward with the Thanksgiving Feast, and Janice had heard from several people who weren't even involved in the committee that they were planning on coming. She was afraid the meeting would turn into one big roast of Zelda. The idea of that would have gutted her at this time yesterday, but given what had happened with Stuart, Janice wasn't even sure she wanted to see Zelda, even if she did have the guts to show up at the meeting.

She left with both Tess and LuAnn. When they arrived at the church, Janice found it difficult to locate a parking spot.

"Looks like a good turnout for the meeting," LuAnn said.

"More like people are curious and want to see what will happen today," Tess countered.

Janice hurried inside with her friends. Though the room was packed, they found three empty seats near the back row and took their places. Charlotte caught her eye and waved, and Janice smiled in return.

She looked around. She didn't see Zelda and decided it was probably better—for everyone involved—if she didn't show up today.

Conversation swirled as Margaret rose and walked toward the front of the room.

"All right, everyone," Margaret said. "Quiet down, now. We've got a lot to get through today." The voices in the room started to quiet, and Margaret waited until they were nearly silent. She was small and looked meek, with her white hair and glasses, but Margaret could still command a room. "Now, as you know, there was a mishap with the donations that were collected at last week's meeting."

"If by mishap, you mean Zelda stole the money, sure."

Janice couldn't see who had called that out, but it sounded like it could have been Thelma Bickerton.

"Now, now," Margaret said. "Let's not repeat the nasty rumors that have been flying around in the press. Zelda McLoughlin was doing her best to fulfill her duties as chair of this committee. The police have not determined what happened to that money, and I will not tolerate any presumptive judgments while I'm chair of this committee."

Janice was surprised to hear this from Margaret. She didn't know if she could be as charitable to Zelda as Margaret was at the moment. Obviously Zelda wasn't the woman Janice had thought she was.

"Our task at the moment is to figure out how to move forward with the meal for next week, if in fact we decide to do so."

"Is there even a question about moving forward?" Mike Vance from Vance Hardware stood in the front row. "If we don't pull this meal together, there are going to be people who don't have a Thanksgiving this year, right?"

"Presumably," Margaret said.

"We can't let that happen," Tama Steele said.

"Yeah. I thought we were all here to volunteer to make sure this happens, not to decide whether or not we want to do it," Wendy Wilson said. "Of course we want to do it."

"If we don't move forward with the meal, what about all those donations we collected all over again this week?" Charlotte said. "I know it's not the full amount that was raised before, but surely it's enough so we can see that people who need it get a meal."

"I can go out and collect more donations," Tess's daughter Lizzie said. Somehow she'd escaped without the triplets today.

"And I'm willing to make a donation," Brad Grimes said. "My original donation was in cash, so it may be gone forever, but I'd rather make another one than think that people in this town might go hungry this Thanksgiving."

"And I'm still willing to donate rolls and pumpkin pies," Sandie from the Better Batter said.

"Plus, Winnie wanted me to let you know that she'll donate a few dozen pecan pies," LuAnn said.

A murmur went through the crowd.

"All right then," Margaret said. "It seems that many people want to move forward with the meal, even if the original bag of donations isn't located. Does that sound right?"

A number of people shouted "yes" or nodded their heads.

"Shall we put it to a vote?" Margaret asked.

A quick vote made the results clear: the Community Thanksgiving Feast would go forward in five days.

Janice teared up at the generosity of her neighbors and friends. Part of her couldn't believe this was really happening. That they were willing to look past the fact that someone had stolen the thousands of dollars they had already collected. She couldn't believe that they would volunteer their time, money, and energy all over again, even when they had already given so much.

But then again, she thought, looking around the room at the people who made up this town, in some ways it wasn't a surprise at all.

CHAPTER TWENTY-EIGHT

November 4, 1859

Prudence woke to Jason gently kissing her forehead. "Prudence, Moses is awake. He is letting me know I am not the one he needs right now." She heard Jason's chuckle over Moses's indignant wails and hastened to his crib. She said nothing as she left the bedroom and settled in the rocker, Moses at her breast. Jason left for the barn and his chores.

She had just laid a sleeping Moses in his crib when she heard a knock on the door.

Silently, carefully, she crept to the front window. A man she didn't know stood on the doorstep.

"Mrs. Willard?" the man called. His clothes were well tended, and he wore a stylish hat. "This is John Paige."

She recognized the name. That was the man Jason had said worked with Miss Fay at the orphanage. But was it truly him? She had no way to know.

"Mrs. Willard," he said, "I'm here to see if Jason and your boy are all right, if they made it back home."

She pulled the door open and joined him on the front porch. "Jason and Moses arrived late last night," she told him. "Perhaps thee could tell me what took them from home?"

Mr. Paige smiled. "I'd be happy to, ma'am." He held his hand out, indicating she should be seated, and she lowered herself to the top step of the porch. He took his hat off and sat down on the other end of the step and leaned against the rail.

John Paige explained what had happened while Prudence was out in the night. A knock had come at the door. Jason had the good sense to hide the infant under the bed before answering the door, praying the whole time that she would not wake up. As he had feared, armed men pushed their way in and looked around the house, but the child did not make a sound. The men found only Moses then vanished into the night, heading off to search the next farm. They said they would be continuing to search the area and warned Jason that if he heard mention of a baby, he would be in violation of the law if he did not report it. But the real message was clear. If Jason was found harboring the child, the law would be the least of his worries.

Jason waited a couple of hours, until he was sure the men were out of the area, then strapped both children to his chest under his coat, saddled Charity, and rode to Catherine Fay's orphanage.

"The child is safe there, ma'am," Mr. Paige said.

Prudence looked up to see Jason coming from the barn.

Mr. Paige glanced up and saw him too. He said softly, "Mrs. Willard, your husband did the only thing he could to save that baby girl. Those men would stop at nothing to get her back."

He stood, stepped off the porch, and held out his hand to Jason. "I'm glad to see you made it home, Jason."

The men shook hands, and after a few moments of quiet conversation, John took his leave, and Jason joined Prudence on the porch.

Prudence finally looked into his eyes and saw only love and forgiveness. She threw her arms around his neck, tears of regret flowing down her face. "Jason...forgive me."

"There is nothing to forgive, my love," he said softly. "Thy heart is tender and noble. I know thee would gladly give every orphan child a home if thee could."

He eased her away so she could see his face. "Catherine has...She found a couple," he said. "A childless couple. They understand the situation and have promised to take the child, to move farther north, and to love the child as their own."

"Oh." It was the best possible scenario, she knew that now. The child would be safe. Safe and free. And Prudence and Jason's family, and the people who worked with them ferrying slaves to freedom, would be safe.

She would have a good life, Prudence knew. She would have parents who loved her, who could provide for her every need. She would not fear that she would be stolen away, taken back to the life that her mother, that poor, brave, selfless woman, had risked everything to free her from. But it still wasn't easy to see her go.

Jason didn't say a word, but put his arms around her again and held her as they watched John Paige disappear down the road. Prudence prayed that God would bless the family, would bless the child, and give her a beautiful life.

A beautiful life, just like she had.

CHAPTER TWENTY-NINE

The days before Thanksgiving flew by, with an inn full of guests and every spare moment going into pulling together the food, decorations, and delivery schedules for the Community Thanksgiving Feast. Janice helped coordinate the deliveries, while Tess served on the task force that would decorate the church with cornucopias, gilt-edged leaves, and bouquets of flowers that definitively did not contain carnations. LuAnn spent much of the time in the kitchen helping Winnie turn out dozens of pecan pies and roasting turkeys to be served at the meal. Charlotte Bickerton had even contributed fat-free kale chips as an appetizer, and Saffron Navratalova had donated a vegan Tofurky to the meal.

Janice didn't know what else to do to find the money that had gone missing. She had come to a brick wall. She had started to accept that it was really and truly gone and that they might never know what had happened to it.

Maybe Zelda really had taken the money after all. It was clear Janice had misjudged her, in any case. If she was capable of dumping Stuart, of dropping him just when he was gearing up to propose, she wasn't the person Janice had thought she was. And, with that realization, she was suddenly seeing everything about Zelda in a new light. Maybe she hadn't actually dropped the bank bag into the deposit box, but had cleverly made it look like she had so she would have an alibi. Maybe this was how she had planned to pay her way into the music world. Was her story about how she got pregnant with Brin even true?

Or maybe it really had been Brin that took the money. Her story about cashing her paychecks and keeping the cash in her car stank like day-old fish. It was entirely possible that she had taken the money from her mom's purse, tossed out the checks, used some of the cash, and tucked the rest in a place where she'd thought no one would find it. Like mother, like daughter, she supposed.

The one silver lining in all this was that she'd gotten to know Ellen better in the past few days, and found she actually liked the young woman. Once you got past the surly attitude—which Janice had come to realize was nothing more than a defensive smoke screen—she was kind and upbeat, and her faith was genuine. She had even volunteered to take over Zelda's food delivery shifts Thanksgiving morning because Zelda was still staying under the radar—for which Janice was grateful. She didn't care to see Zelda anytime soon, if ever again.

Ellen had moved back to Zelda's because the inn was booked during the Thanksgiving weekend, and Janice found that she kind of missed her.

Janice distracted herself by pouring everything she had into preparing for the big day, as well as making a big dish of her traditional corn pudding for her own dinner with Stuart and Stacy and Larry. Stuart didn't think he could face the community gathering with all its memories of Zelda, so he and Janice were going to Stacy's once all the deliveries were made.

She was just taking the corn pudding out of the oven when LuAnn came into the kitchen. "That smells delicious! I'm going to have to steal a taste before you wrap it up for tomorrow," she said.

Janice handed her a fork. "Here, you can take a bite now. You know you're welcome to join us at Stacy's if you want to."

"I know," LuAnn said, taking the fork from her. "But I want to experience the whole Thanksgiving Feast. It's my first one, you know." She took a bite of the corn. "Mmm…just as good as it smells." She put the fork in the sink. "Do you have any idea what Zelda and Brin are doing tomorrow? Do you think they'll be at the church?"

Janice tore the aluminum foil from its roll with a bit more force than necessary. "I don't know, and I don't really care," she said.

LuAnn frowned and folded her arms across her chest. Janice could see she'd put on her "teacher" face that Tess teased her about. "I think you're letting your disappointment about Stuart's engagement take you to a dark place, girlfriend," she said.

Janice felt her stomach burn. "It's not just disappointment. She's really hurt Stuart. I don't know if I can be her friend anymore."

LuAnn didn't back down. "I remember reading something in Prudence's journal I think might be good for you to read," she said. "I remember the date because she wrote it on November fourth, which is my mother's birthday." Her face softened, and she reached to touch Janice's arm. "Promise me you'll read it, today, okay? I think you might be glad you did."

Janice humphed. "Okay, I'll read it," she said. "But I won't make any promises about that woman."

LuAnn laughed. "I think sometimes I know you better than you know yourself, Janice Eastman. Just read it, and we'll see. November 4, 1859."

Janice finished cleaning the kitchen and went upstairs to retrieve her copy of Prudence's journal. She made a cup of tea, settled in her armchair, and opened the journal to November 4, 1859.

"Charity suffereth long, and is kind; charity envieth not; charity vaunteth not itself, is not puffed up, doth not behave itself unseemly, seeketh not her own, is not easily provoked, thinketh no evil; rejoiceth not in iniquity, but rejoiceth in the truth; beareth all things, believeth all things, hopeth all things, endureth all things." The Lord teaches us that in I Corinthians 13, and I certainly committed these verses to memory as a child and carried the words in my heart as if I knew exactly what they meant.

Today those words pierce my heart and expose my guilt. My tears blur the page as I think of how I misjudged my beloved Jason. How could I have thought the worst of him? How could I have accused him of wrong motives? My love is a weak and poor thing if it proves faithless in the face of doubt; such a love does not come from the One who never gives up on me even when the rest of the world would do so. It is He who shows me the heart of a true friend. How I long to possess that heart!

Before she reached the end of the passage, Janice's eyes had filled with tears and her heart with conviction. "Forgive me, Lord," she whispered. "I haven't been a friend to Zelda; I've doubted her word and made accusations against her to others." She found a tissue in her pocket and blew her nose. "Help me exchange my feelings of disappointment and anger for love and loyalty, and give me the words Zelda needs to hear to encourage her and let her know she's not alone." She reached for her cell phone and punched Zelda's number.

Thirty minutes later she ended the call, wrung out but content, having gotten and given forgiveness. And she was utterly convinced of Zelda's innocence in the case of the missing money.

She left her sitting room to pour some more tea and met LuAnn in the kitchenette. LuAnn took one look at her and wrapped her arms around Janice in a tight hug. Janice just hugged her back, so grateful that she had friends who loved her enough to hold her feet to the fire when she messed up.

By the time she fell into bed Wednesday night, Janice was exhausted, but sleep was evasive, as it had been so often lately. She was so tired her eyelids felt heavy, but as soon as she lay down, the worries started up. Worries about Stuart, that his heartbreak would make him bitter, that he'd never find someone to love who deserved his love in return. Worries about the logistics all running smoothly tomorrow. Worries that she wasn't doing enough, wasn't good enough. That she'd failed.

That was the one she couldn't stop from looping over and over in her mind. That she and her friends had not managed to solve this mystery. The Thanksgiving Feast was going forward anyway, but the money had never been recovered. They hadn't been able to find it.

Scenes from the past week and a half played over in her mind. The security footage where you could see Zelda open the deposit box. The shot of Jessica reaching her arm down into the deposit box, searching for mail.

Then a new thought occurred to her. Hadn't Jessica said...? Wait. She played back the conversation with Jessica in her mind.

And then, she thought back to the inside of the night deposit box. She hadn't been able to see the top of the box, because of the underside of the lid. But, surely, someone would have noticed if...

If only those security cameras had been working. You might have been able to see inside the box, even just a quick glimpse, from those cameras. If it hadn't been for those pranksters who had broken the cameras. Who had tagged the walls, and shoved fish in through the mail slot, who had put a firecracker in...

Wait. Janice closed her eyes, trying to picture it. The inside of the deposit box. The lid bowed in...

Was there any way?

Janice slowly sat up in bed. It was a long shot, she knew. A Hail Mary, if there ever was one. But now that she'd thought of it, she couldn't stop wondering.

She pushed the covers off and stepped out of bed. She didn't even bother to take her nightgown off, she just slipped a pair of pants on under it and a sweatshirt on over it, and then she grabbed her purse and crept out of her room.

"What are you doing?" Tess was dumping mini marshmallows on top of a sweet potato casserole. She was planning to eat with Lizzie and her family and Jeff Jr. after she worked at the church, and she'd promised to bring this dish, which her children loved when they were little.

"I didn't know anyone was still up."

"Clearly, or you wouldn't have come out of your room dressed like that." She settled the last few marshmallows on top of the casserole with her fingers. "Where are you headed?"

"I had an idea," Janice said.

"Oh, dear."

"It's kind of crazy."

"I would assume nothing less, judging by your outfit."

"I'm going to the bank."

"At this hour?"

Janice hesitated. "Maybe it's best to do this at this hour, honestly."

"Do what?"

"I just want to take a closer look at that night deposit box." Janice slipped her feet into the boots that were by the door.

"And it can't wait until daylight?"

"I don't think I'm going to be able sleep until I check this out."

"Okay." Tess sighed. "Hang on. Let me grab my coat."

"You don't have to come."

"Oh yes I do. Who knows what kind of trouble you're going to get into, and you'll need help talking your way out of it. You might even need someone to pay your bail."

"I'm not going to—"

But Tess had already vanished into her room, and she reappeared a few minutes later wearing her coat and carrying her purse. She ducked her head into LuAnn's room, but she was already asleep. Just as well, Janice thought, since one of them needed to be on hand during the night in case a guest needed help.

"So why are we going to look at the deposit box in the middle of the night?" Tess asked as they drove through the quiet town. The lights in the houses and businesses were off, and the streetlights cast a warm glow over the empty streets.

"I want to look at the inside."

"We already looked at it, remember? You and LuAnn had to convince the bank manager in the process."

"I want to see it from the outside though."

"Okay…" It was clear Tess thought she was nuts. And maybe she was. But she just had this hunch, this gut feeling that there was something they were missing, and it had to do with the night deposit box.

They parked in the empty bank lot and hurried across the pavement. The temperature had dropped, and a bitter wind whipped through the night air. Janice pulled the handle of the deposit box, and it swung open.

"Can you use your phone's flashlight to light up the inside?"

She looked back over her shoulder and saw that Tess was doing some kind of strange dance.

"What are you doing?"

"Flossing."

"What?" What was she even talking about?

"All the kids are doing it these days."

"Okay. But why are you doing it right now?"

"I'm trying to distract whoever watches this security video from whatever it is you're about to do. Whatever it is you're about to do while still in your nightgown, I might add. You'll thank me when you don't end up in prison because they were too awed by my flossing skills."

Most of the time Janice loved Tess's sense of humor, but right now she wasn't in the mood. "Tess. Can you please get over here and help me?"

Tess grumbled, but she walked over, pulled out her phone, and shone it into the open night deposit box.

"What exactly are you looking for?"

"I'm not sure." Janice twisted her arm to try to get it into the deposit box, but she couldn't feel very far down. Still, she ran her hand along the cold metal, feeling every inch, looking for...she didn't really know. A hidden compartment, or a secret button, or something. Whatever it was that had cut Jessica Landry's arm. But there was nothing. At least, not in the section that she could feel.

"We'd better get going," Tess said as headlights swept into the parking lot. Janice looked up and saw that it was a police car.

"Whoops." She closed the slot, but Officer Randy Lewis was already stepping out of the police car. Janice felt a strange rush of gratitude that it was him. She'd taught his Sunday school class years ago, and he was more likely to be lenient toward them than another officer.

"Can I ask what you're doing, Mrs. Eastman?" Randy asked as he crossed the parking lot. His boots thudded against the pavement.

"I was just...I mean, I was...You wouldn't believe me if I said I was making a deposit, would you?"

"No," he said. "And I know that's not what you're going to say, since you're the one that told me twenty years ago that God doesn't like it when we lie."

Busted. "I was just checking something," she said lamely.

"Is that why your whole arm was in the night deposit box?" he asked.

"I was...I hoped..." Janice's words were getting tangled. And she realized that she looked ridiculous, with the lacy edge of her flannel nightgown peeking out from under her coat.

"Should I assume this has something to do with the missing money?" Randy asked.

"That's right." Tess was somehow calm enough to speak clearly.

"I'm real sorry about that," he said. "But I'm going to have to ask you to move along."

Janice knew better than to argue. She and Tess hurried to the car.

"Happy Thanksgiving!" Tess called out just before she ducked inside. Randy waved, and then he sat and watched them as they buckled in and pulled out of the parking lot.

"Well, did you find anything?" Tess asked.

"No," Janice said, shaking her head. "It was a big waste of time. If there's anything there, I didn't find it."

For some reason, this made her feel more hopeless than ever.

CHAPTER THIRTY

J anice was up early Thursday morning and headed over to the church, her car loaded down with food. Two roasted turkeys that would be cut up and delivered to those who couldn't attend the meal were resting in the trunk, and the back seat was covered with utensils and dishes for the main meal that would be served in the church. The church kitchen was already full of women scurrying around, and dishes of food covered every available surface. There were dozens of turkeys, piles of mashed potatoes, huge baskets full of rolls and bread. There was so much stuffing that they'd had to use the giant soup pots to hold it all. It was messy and chaotic, and, to Janice's eye, it was beautiful. The body of Christ in action.

"Oh, set those here," Chelsea Penny said, clearing a space for the serving dishes. Chelsea owned Nacho Average Taco and had signed up to help pull together the food for the on-site meal today.

"Okay," Janice said. "There are two turkeys in my trunk."

"Nick and Zack, can you go get those?" Chelsea gestured to her two teenage sons who had been loafing in the corner. They turned and hurried up the stairs.

"Thank you," Janice said.

Chelsea shrugged. "It keeps them out of trouble."

"This is amazing," Janice said, taking in the mountains of food and the dozens of people scurrying to make it all come together.

"It's going to be a great day," Chelsea said and then turned as Marla Still came down the stairs balancing a dish of sweet potatoes in her hands. "You can set that right here," Chelsea called. Soon, Janice was swept up in the chaos, and she and Wendy Wilson worked on packaging deliveries into Styrofoam coolers. She caught periodic glimpses of LuAnn and her "special" friend, Brad Grimes. They were carving the turkeys.

"This one has sweet potatoes, rolls, mashed potatoes, stuffing, and turkey," Wendy said. They had packed each dish into disposable plastic containers and given each delivery a significant helping of turkey. "It's missing cranberry sauce and dessert."

"Coming right up." Janice handed Wendy a container of cranberry sauce, homemade by Ruby Meyers, and balanced one of Winnie's pecan pies on top. Braced against the side of the cooler, it would stay in place.

"Great. This one's ready to go." Wendy hoisted the cooler and handed it to Jeff Jr., Tess's son, who carried it to the table by the door where Becky Eberly was attaching names and addresses to each cooler and assigning them to a driver for delivery.

"Hi, Janice."

Janice looked up to see Ellen coming across the basement toward her. "Hi there, Ellen. Thanks for coming today." Janice saw that Ellen had dressed up for the occasion and was wearing a nice wool sweater over her jeans.

"I'm happy to help." She looked around. "I'm supposed to take over Zelda's deliveries. Who do I talk to about that?"

"Becky Eberly, over there in the corner, will get you squared away. She's the one in the brown sweater."

"Great. Thanks."

"Did you get your car working?" When Brin had picked Ellen up from the inn on Monday, Ellen had vowed that she was going to get her car fixed so she wouldn't have to rely on others for transportation any longer.

"Sadly, no." Ellen grimaced. "It turns out it needs a whole new transmission, which, well…let's just say I almost wish I had stolen that money, because that's the only way I'm going to be able to afford that."

Janice laughed, and it felt good to realize that she could find humor in something so terrible.

"So are you planning to deliver the meals on your bike? I heard Charlotte Bickerton say she and Paul were planning to try to make their deliveries that way."

Ellen laughed. "No. It's twenty-five degrees out there. I'll use a car, thank you very much. Zelda let me borrow hers."

"That was nice of her."

Ellen shrugged. "Considering she was supposed to be making these deliveries herself, I don't know whether it's nice or if she just felt bad." She jiggled the keys in her hand. "Then again, she may very well wish she'd just made the deliveries herself by the time I'm done here. Her car is a stick shift, and I'm mediocre at best driving stick. Pray for me."

"I'll pray for everyone on the roads today," Janice said with a smile. And then, a moment later, she asked, "How is she doing?"

"She's doing okay," Ellen said. "She told me your call made her feel a lot better. She ate something yesterday, so that's progress."

Oh, dear. She'd read that convicting journal entry none too soon.

"Yeah, she's still in no shape to be here today. She's embarrassed, of course, but she's also kind of a zombie. Not eating, not really sleeping. Forget about showering. I think she's still in shock, to be honest. Everything she thought she had, her career, people she loved, just gone, like that." Ellen snapped her fingers. "It's going to take her some time."

"Stuart would have stood by her," Janice said. "He believes her." She choked up. "I believe her."

"I know that, and you know that," Ellen said. "But I think she's just feeling like she really let him down."

Janice wanted to argue that Zelda had only let Stuart down when she refused to let him help her, but she bit her tongue. It wouldn't help anything to argue with Ellen. Ellen saw the truth just as clearly as Janice did.

"I can't help but think she'll come around," Ellen said quietly. "She loves him. I can see that. She hasn't stopped loving him. I think she just needs some time to make sense of everything that's happened."

"I hope you're right," Janice said.

"Well, wish me luck." Ellen smiled. "Pray I don't crash and spill turkeys all over town."

"I will pray for that." Janice leaned in and gave Ellen a hug, and then she turned back to filling coolers. In the next hour, they had all the packaged meals out for delivery, and everyone turned their attention to getting the community meal ready to serve upstairs in the sanctuary.

Round tables had been set up throughout the sanctuary, which seemed bigger without the pews. Each table was anchored by a centerpiece of zinnias, daisies, and mums—not a carnation in sight—draped around cornucopias, and the mismatched tableware, gathered from so many homes and businesses in town, looked delightfully intentional. Colored light filtered through the stained glass windows, casting patches of blue and red and green over the white tablecloths. Janice studied the window that had always been her favorite, the one that showed Christ as the Good Shepherd with a lamb draped over His shoulders. If God cared for that little lost lamb, how much more must He care for her? Janice had spent so many Sunday mornings staring at that picture, and she never got tired of it.

"It's gorgeous, isn't it?" Tess asked, coming up behind her.

"It is beautiful," Janice said. "It always has been."

She had so many memories tied up in this space. So many Thanksgiving meals shared with friends and neighbors. So many Sunday mornings, sitting in the front row, watching Lawrence preach. So many weddings, funerals, baptisms. So many major life events threaded through with countless small, everyday moments. So many images of Lawrence, serving tirelessly, pointing people toward God. Janice bit her lip.

Without a word, Tess reached out and took her hand and squeezed it.

"I should get going," Janice finally said as Tama Pearson started carrying trays of rolls and potatoes up from the basement. She wasn't quite ready to face whatever might come out if she let herself stand here and reminisce for much longer. Tess gave her a knowing look, and then she let her pull away. "I'm supposed to be at Stacy's in an hour, and I still have to finish the corn casserole."

"Have a good time with your kids," Tess said. She wasn't headed over to Lizzie's until later.

"You too," Janice said. She slipped on her coat, grabbed her purse, and headed for the door.

Janice was a tiny bit sad she wasn't staying for the community meal, but she was looking forward to seeing Stacy, Larry, and Stuart. Poor Stuart...Her heart dropped, thinking about the look on his face when he'd given back the ring. He loved Zelda, that much was clear. He loved her, and he always had. Maybe he always would, though Janice hoped he would find a way to put this heartbreak behind him. For all of them to put it behind them, she thought. She loved Zelda and had expected her to become her daughter. She had to mourn the loss of that expectation too.

Janice drove home and parked in the driveway. She'd started to walk up toward the inn when her phone started to ring. She dug her phone out of her purse and looked at the screen.

Ellen.

"Hello?" Janice put the phone to her ear. "Ellen." She heard a siren wailing in the background. "Is everything all right?"

"Hi, Janice. I'm sorry to bother you, but there's been... I kind of had a little accident, and—"

"Oh, my goodness. Are you all right? Where are—"

"I'm okay," Ellen said as the sirens got louder. "I'm not hurt. It's just that... Well, I think you should come down here."

"Where are you?"

"I'm at the bank. I think there's something you should see."

CHAPTER THIRTY-ONE

When Janice pulled into the bank parking lot a few minutes later, police cars and an ambulance surrounded the side of the building, which had a gaping hole in the stone facade. As Janice got closer, she saw that Zelda's car was up on the sidewalk, its nose buried in the building. And there was Ellen, talking to Chief Mayfield, using a lot of hand gestures to explain what had happened.

"Ellen." Janice climbed out of her car and ran toward her. "Are you all right?"

Shattered glass littered the ground, and the front end of the car was crushed. The bumper lay on the ground, and a hot metallic odor hung in the air. The airbag had deployed and now hung limply around the front seat.

"Hi, Janice." Ellen turned toward her, and Chief Mayfield nodded, seeing her approach. "I'm okay. I'm not hurt. I'm just, you know. I just crashed Zelda's car into the building, so it's not my best day ever."

"What happened?" Ellen had been out delivering turkeys. She wasn't supposed to be anywhere near the bank. What was she even doing in this part of town?

"Hang on," Ellen said as another car pulled into the parking lot. A blue Jeep with a flower decal on the back. Janice froze as Zelda stepped out. She'd lost weight, and there were dark circles under her eyes. Her skin was sallow, and her hair hung in a greasy ponytail. Janice didn't know why she was surprised. She should have known Zelda would come. It was her car that had just landed nose-deep in the bank, after all.

"Hi, Zelda," Janice said, and Zelda gave her a weak smile. Janice felt a rush of love go through her. Yes, she still loved Zelda like a daughter—no matter what.

Zelda rushed to pull Ellen into her arms. "Are you hurt?"

Chief Mayfield stepped back.

"I'm okay," Ellen said, and then she started to cry as Zelda hugged her tightly. "I'm so sorry about your car. I didn't mean... I'm so sorry. I'll pay you back. It's my fault, I—"

"I'm not worried about any of that," Zelda said. "I'm just worried about you. Are you sure you're not hurt? You should go to the hospital and get checked out." She gestured toward the waiting ambulance. The EMTs stood by, waiting, as did several police officers.

"I'm not hurt. I just—I don't know what happened."

She was probably in shock, Janice thought. And she should go to the hospital. The airbag had no doubt prevented the worst of the damage, but she could still be hurt where they couldn't see it.

After a few more moments of hugging, Ellen pulled back, tears in her eyes. "Okay, so as I was explaining to this police guy"—Chief Mayfield maintained a stoic look, even though Janice knew he had to have a reaction to that—"I was out delivering my meals. And I was thinking about how I know Zelda put that money in the deposit slot and how it vanished and how everything has been awful for her ever since." She turned to Zelda. "I mean, no offense, but you're a mess."

Zelda started to argue but then must have thought better of it because she let her continue.

"So, I don't really know what I was thinking, but I decided to come here and just you know, check it out. Maybe see if seeing it again would spark some kind of memory about what had happened to the money. Only, I was distracted, and, well, the three pedals kind of threw me off for a minute there. I just hit the wrong pedal." She sighed. "I warned you I wasn't very good at driving stick."

"It's all right," Zelda said again, and started to move in to give her another hug, but Ellen held up her hand.

"Hang on. There's more." Ellen shook her head. "So, obviously, I was kind of stunned after plowing into the bank. I sat in the car for a minute, trying to figure out if I was dead or what. But when I finally got out, I looked around and tried to figure out how much damage I'd caused."

It was a lot, Janice thought. But at least Ellen was safe. The Lord had been watching over her.

"And I noticed this." Ellen started to walk toward the building, but Chief Mayfield stopped her.

"We need to wait until Paul Townsend gets here," he said.

That didn't stop Janice from turning to look. The stone around the overnight deposit box had crumbled, and the box itself was warped. She could see the same thing she'd seen from inside the bank—that the top was bowed and dipped in the middle.

Ellen gave him a sour look and then turned to Janice and Zelda. "I guess we have to wait. But I didn't wait before. I looked, and I noticed that the box is all bent."

Janice nodded. After two tons of steel had rammed into it, she had no doubt it was bent.

As if reading her mind, Ellen shook her head. "No, it was bent before. I know, because I found something above it. It was jammed on top of the box. You would never have known it was there."

"Wait. Do you mean—" Zelda started.

"The bank bag," Ellen confirmed. "The one that everyone thought I stole? That you stole?" She looked at Zelda. "It's been on top of the night deposit box this whole time."

Janice looked, but from where she was, she couldn't see much beyond a twisted mess.

A hundred questions ran through her mind. Was it true? How could Ellen be sure it was the same bag? How was it possible that it could have been there the whole time?

Ellen continued to fill them in on the details of the accident, but all Janice could think was, if this was true, she'd been right. If she was right—and if Ellen was telling the truth, and Janice thought she probably was—the deposit box had gotten damaged when the firecracker had been put inside it, but no one had realized it. Zelda hadn't known that, because the blast had bowed the top of the box, she would have had to angle the bag downward as she pushed it through the slot. She'd pushed it straight in, and it had missed the slot and gotten wedged on top of the box.

And if the bag had gotten wedged on top of the box, that meant that Zelda hadn't stolen the money after all. It meant that none of them had. Zelda could probably get her contract back. Maybe she and Stuart could even—

Janice knew she was getting ahead of herself here. But for the first time in several days, she felt a thrill of hope.

Paul Townsend arrived a few minutes later, and after he had a conference with Chief Mayfield, they examined the damage and the night deposit box. And then, as Janice held her breath, he reached his arm in and pulled out a black bank bag.

Zelda let out a cry that would stay with Janice forever. Somewhere between relief, joy, and excitement, it meant that she was free. Janice walked over and pulled Zelda into her arms. Zelda leaned on her and cried, and Janice held her up. This felt right, she thought. A part of her would always consider Zelda her daughter, no matter what happened with Stuart.

When Zelda finally pulled back, it was to turn to Ellen. "You need to go to the hospital. Get checked out."

"I don't think—"

"I don't care. Go. Those guys are waiting to take you." She pointed to the EMTs, still standing by the ambulance. "I will be along shortly."

Ellen must have seen that Zelda meant business, because she nodded and walked over to the EMTs without any other argument. Once she was on her way, Zelda and Janice climbed into Janice's car to wait. She turned on the engine and cranked up the heater, and praise music played softly in the background. There were so many things Janice wanted to say to

Zelda, so many things she wanted to ask, but mostly they sat in silence, watching the drama unfold in front of them. Janice texted Stacy to say she'd be later than expected, and she texted Tess and LuAnn to let them know what was going on. Janice knew she should probably get those meals out of the back of Zelda's car and deliver them on Ellen's behalf. The Thanksgiving Feast was probably already underway. But she didn't leave. There was no way she was going to miss this.

It took a good long while for Paul to open the bank bag and verify its contents and to examine the night deposit box all over again. But finally, he walked over to Janice's car and gestured for Zelda to step out. Janice stepped out of her side and listened as Paul confirmed that it was the missing bank bag, and that it had somehow gotten stuck on top of the night deposit box. By the time he was finished, both Janice and Zelda had tears rolling down their cheeks.

"That's it, then," Janice said. "That's proof. You made that deposit. You're free."

Zelda, tears staining her cheeks, nodded. Then she threw her arms around Janice again and wept.

CHAPTER THIRTY-TWO

Janice had assumed it would take Stuart a while to get over what had happened. To regain trust in Zelda after she'd dumped him. But Stuart, God bless his loyal heart, had immediately taken her back when Zelda came to him the day after Thanksgiving to apologize. He told Zelda that he understood why she'd done it, and he forgave her. He trusted that she would never walk away from him again.

Saturday morning dawned clear and cold, and Jeff Jr. showed up bright and early to drive the truck to the Christmas parade. The ladies had decorated the back with the Christmas quilt and had strung evergreen boughs and fairy lights along the sides. A wreath hung on the front. They would sit in the back, bundled up in more layers than Janice cared to count, and toss mini candy canes at the children along the parade route. And, as a special, late-breaking addition, Zelda would be riding with them, singing Christmas carols.

"Are you ready to go?" LuAnn asked. She looked like a snowman, buried under so many layers of clothing.

"As ready as I'll ever be," Janice said. "Remind me. Why did sitting in the back of a truck in thirty-something degree weather seem like a good idea?"

"Because it's fun," LuAnn said. She handed Janice the red wool hat that matched her own. They were all going to match, which Janice supposed was a nice touch.

"And because it's good exposure for the inn," Tess added.

"Just as long as we don't die from exposure," Janice said.

They greeted many of their neighbors and friends as Jeff Jr. drove the truck into their place at the staging area for the parade. Chief Mayfield was dressed as Santa Claus, and his red convertible, decorated as a sleigh, would be the last float down the parade route.

"Over here!" Tess called. She was waving her arms and gesturing for Zelda. Zelda smiled and threaded her way through the people waiting for the parade to start moving.

"This looks great," Zelda said. LuAnn held out a hand and helped her climb into the truck.

"Thank you for doing this," Janice said, pulling her in for a hug.

"Thank you for asking me," Zelda said. "And, well, for everything you did these past couple of weeks. All of you."

"We knew you were innocent," Tess said. "Will you be able to get your recording contract back?"

"Yes, Clive thinks it's very likely." Zelda smiled. "The paperwork hadn't gone through yet, so it wasn't difficult to stop it. And the label seemed to be satisfied once they saw the headline in yesterday's paper."

"That's so good to hear." Yesterday's *Marietta Times* had printed the whole story about how the bank bag had been found. It declared that Zelda had been wrongly accused and had been cleared of all charges.

"Nothing is final yet, but I'm hopeful," Zelda said.

"We'll be praying," Janice promised, and Zelda leaned in and gave her a hug. Janice would also be praying that she and Stuart would have wisdom as they moved forward in their relationship.

"This is fun," LuAnn said as they got into their places. Zelda stood at the front of the truck bed, nearest to the cab, and held a battery-powered microphone, while Janice, LuAnn, and Tess settled in around the truck bed, each with a bag of candy canes to toss out.

"Are you ready?" Jeff Jr. called, leaning out the open front door.

"Ready," Tess called to her son.

And then, slowly, they began to move through the streets of town. The streetlamps were already decorated with tinsel, and lighted decorations were hung over the streets. Zelda sang Christmas favorites, like "Hark! The Herald Angels Sing" and "O Come, All Ye Faithful." Janice tossed out candy canes to children along the route and waved at friends and neighbors all up and down the streets. She waved to friends from church and people who'd known Lawrence and people who had come into her life only recently. She waved like a maniac when she saw Stacy and Larry and Tess's grandchildren Henry, Liam, and Harper. By the time they rolled into the grocery store parking lot that marked the end of the parade route, Janice's bag of candy was empty, but her heart was full.

"Well, that was fun," she said and started to push herself up. But she froze when she saw Stuart walking toward the truck, a small black velvet pouch in hand. Janice's heart started pounding. Was this real? Was he really going to do it?

Zelda was tucking her microphone into its carrying case and hadn't seemed to notice Stuart approaching yet, but Tess and LuAnn had. They both looked at Janice, and Janice nodded. As quickly and as gracefully as possible, the three of them hurried out of the truck bed, leaving just Zelda standing against the background of the Christmas quilt.

"Is he about to do what I think he is?" LuAnn whispered. Janice shrugged but watched as her son climbed up into the bed of the truck. Zelda's face broke out in a wide smile, and Janice saw it then. Zelda loved Stuart, through and through. It was there in her eyes. Zelda would care for him, stand by him, love him, till the end of her days.

Zelda's smile turned to confusion as Stuart got down on one knee, and then, to laughter.

"Zelda McLoughlin, you are the love of my life," Stuart declared. "I have always loved you, ever since we were teenagers, and I will love you until the day I die. I love the way you serve God with your whole heart. I love the way you lead others to love God through your music. I want to stand by your side as you worship and serve the Lord the rest of your days. Zelda, I know this is fast, and I know you weren't expecting this. But I let you get away from me once, and this time, I want to ask you to marry me before it's too late."

Zelda was crying now, as was Janice. And, she realized, Tess and LuAnn were both dabbing at their eyes as well.

"Zelda," he said, pulling the ruby engagement ring out of the bag. "Will you marry me?"

Zelda didn't hesitate. "Yes!" she shrieked, and Janice might have shrieked a little bit too. Zelda held out her left hand, and Stuart carefully placed the golden band around her fourth finger.

"It's gorgeous," Zelda said. "Did you pick this out all by yourself?"

"It belonged to my grandmother," Stuart said, shaking his head. "I was hoping—if you don't like it, we can…But I thought—"

"I love it," Zelda said. "It's perfect."

She held the ring up, and it caught the light, and then Zelda leaned forward and kissed Stuart. Around them, people started cheering, and Janice realized that Stuart's proposal had attracted quite an audience. With tears in her eyes, Janice started to clap and cheer too.

He'd finally done it. Stuart had finally proposed to Zelda. And, Janice thought, laughing, she wouldn't have to worry anymore about accidentally spilling the beans. For that, and for a thousand other reasons, she couldn't be more thankful.

Yes, she thought, looking around at the people gathered to celebrate the coming Christmas season. She had so much to be thankful for. For the business that she loved. For dear friends who felt more like family. For a town that looked out for its own. And for her children, and now, for Zelda and Brin. She had a granddaughter now, she realized with a shiver of excitement. And, hopefully soon, several others that would come along in the next few years.

She was blessed, richly, deeply, and truly. And she planned to enjoy it all for every moment the Lord gave her.

Dear Reader,

Thank you for joining LuAnn, Tess, Janice—and me!—as the mystery of the missing bank bag was solved. Contrary to what some readers might think, many mystery writers get all the way to the end of the book before they determine which of their cast of characters to pick as the culprit. Yes, it's true! I had so many potential culprits in mind when I began writing *Before It's Too Late* that I had a hard time eliminating the ones who could not have committed the crime. Finally, I settled on the culprit, which wasn't a culprit at all but rather a malfunctioning night deposit box. Were you surprised too, or did you guess correctly? If so, congratulations! You're a great sleuth!

In addition to the contemporary story of the Inn Crowd, there is a more serious aspect to the Wayfarers Inn series. I am honored to tell the story, however fictional, of just a few of the people who toiled invisibly along the stations of the Underground Railroad. While most of their names have been lost to time, the efforts of those who risked their lives to deliver precious souls from the horror of slavery should never be forgotten.

This is my third mystery to write in the Wayfarers Inn series, and this one came with some particularly difficult challenges. The unexpected loss of my son Andrew Y'Barbo came during the final stages of writing this story and, as you can imagine, I was completely derailed and left drifting for a period of time. My Guideposts family, especially my amazing editor Susan Downs, rallied around me and offered love, encouragement, prayers, and so much more. Thanks solely to Susan and the Guideposts family, this book is in your hands today. I owe these amazing people a debt of gratitude I will never be able to repay.

Again, thank you for taking this journey with me. I hope you'll join LuAnn, Tess, and Janice next time for another mystery and adventure at Wayfarers Inn. I can't wait to see what kind of trouble the Inn Crowd gets mixed up in. Can you?

Enjoy!

Signed,

Kathleen Y'Barbo

ABOUT THE AUTHOR

Best-selling author Kathleen Y'Barbo is a multiple Carol Award and RITA nominee and bestselling author of more than ninety books with almost two million copies of her books in print in the US and abroad. A tenth-generation Texan and certified paralegal, she has been nominated for a Career Achievement Award as well as a Reader's Choice Award and several Top Picks by *Romantic Times* magazine. She is a member of American Christian Fiction Writers, Novelists Inc., and the State Bar of Texas Paralegal Division.

To find out more about Kathleen or connect with her through social media, check out her website at kathleenybarbo .com.

THANKSGIVING AT THE LAFAYETTE

The Community Thanksgiving Feast in our story may be fictional, but events just like it take place all throughout the Ohio River Valley during the Thanksgiving season. One of these Thanksgiving buffets is held in the Lafayette Hotel in Marietta.

The Lafayette Hotel is named for the Marquis de Lafayette, the French hero of the Revolutionary War. A plaque nearby marks the spot where the Marquis reportedly came ashore in Marietta in 1825. But before the hotel bore this hero's name, it was the Bellevue Hotel.

Built in 1892, the Bellevue boasted four stories, fifty-five steam-heated rooms, and a call bell system in every room, among other features that were modern to that time. A single night's stay would run you a whopping—are you ready for it?—two to three dollars!

Unfortunately, the Bellevue burned down on April 26, 1916, and pictures of the blaze are displayed in the Lafayette's Gunroom Restaurant. On July 1, 1918, the newly rebuilt and renamed Lafayette Hotel opened in the spot where the Bellevue once stood.

The Lafayette is a great place to reflect on the history of those who have gone before us, and to be thankful for the blessings their lives allow us to enjoy.

Mimi's Thanksgiving Chocolate Cake

Cake Ingredients:

½ cup vegetable oil

½ cup water

3 tablespoons cocoa powder

2 cups sugar

1 teaspoon vanilla

½ cup buttermilk

1 teaspoon baking soda

2 eggs, beaten

2 cups flour

Frosting Ingredients:

½ stick butter

3 tablespoons cocoa powder

6 tablespoons milk

1 small box powdered sugar, sifted

1 teaspoon vanilla

Cake: Preheat oven to 350 degrees. Mix together oil, water, cocoa powder, sugar, and vanilla in medium sauce pan and heat until sugar dissolves. Add buttermilk and soda and beat together until smooth. Add eggs one at a time and then add flour. Beat well and pour into greased 9 × 13-inch pan for 30 minutes, until a toothpick comes out clean. Remove from oven and frost immediately.

Frosting: Heat together butter, cocoa powder, and milk in medium saucepan over low heat until butter is melted. Add powdered sugar and vanilla and mix well. Pour over hot cake and let cool.

Enjoy!

Read on for a sneak peek of another exciting book
in the Secrets of Wayfarers Inn series!

MERCY'S SONG
by Candice Prentice

Two thoughts occupied LuAnn Sherrill's mind as she stepped out of Jeremiah's Coffee House with two lattes and a breakfast wrap. The first was the Marietta Christmas in History Home Tour, for which she'd recently been asked to step in as chairwoman.

The second was the imminent arrival at the Greyhound bus station of one of her favorite past students, Jerri Carrington—the person for whom LuAnn had bought breakfast.

LuAnn hummed "Silent Night" as she walked to her car. Abnormally cold wind buffeted her head. Christmas wreaths hung on the lampposts, reminding her of the finishing touches on the Christmas decor still left to complete at her home and business, Wayfarers Inn.

She glanced at her watch. Normally at this time of day, she was at the inn, working the breakfast rush, along with her best friends and co-owners, Tess Wallace and Janice Eastman. They had graciously covered for her so she could pick up Jerri.

"LuAnn, wait!"

LuAnn turned. Fern McPherson, one of the Christmas tour committee members, hustled up the sidewalk toward her, plump legs churning and heels clomping on the cement.

"Good morning." LuAnn gritted her teeth as a burst of arctic air blasted past her.

Fern stopped two feet in front of LuAnn, reached into her purse, which was the size of a shopping bag, and pulled out her leather-bound notebook, waving it in the air.

LuAnn backed up in surprise.

"I've made a new list," Fern said.

"About what?" Lists were one thing she and Fern had in common, but Fern took list making to a whole new level. As she swirled her notebook in the air like some sort of conductor's baton, LuAnn couldn't help but notice the exquisite floral tooling on the cover.

"I'm checking on the people whose homes are part of the tour. Yesterday afternoon I went to see the Bickerton sisters to check on their progress. They wouldn't let me in the house."

LuAnn's gaze snapped back to Fern. "You what? Uh, they are, uh—"

"Eccentric." Fern waved her notebook again, eyes glinting. "I'll be checking in with the Aldriches today. I assume Wayfarers Inn will be prepared for the tour, and I won't need to check it."

LuAnn eyed Fern with concern. "At the previous meeting we agreed that I would check in with everyone later this week, after the final committee meeting."

Fern shrugged, hitched her purse strap closer to her neck, and squinted at LuAnn. "I wasn't at the last meeting or the meeting before that, and no one consulted me. Besides, one person shouldn't be running the whole show."

LuAnn struggled to find words that might take some of the fire out of Fern's eyes. "None of us is solely running the show. We're working as a team."

Fern sniffed and ignored her. "In addition, I'll be at the final committee meeting tonight to protest this ridiculous idea of non-paying participants."

"We discussed the idea at the meeting two weeks ago. Everyone voted to approve. I handed out fliers to local businesses to advertise. Surely you saw one of those. After the main event on Saturday, the host houses will be open for two hours on Sunday afternoon so people from the community can look at the decorations and lights. But desserts and lectures won't be included. It's a good community outreach."

Fern slapped her notebook on her free hand. "I should have been consulted."

LuAnn shivered, and she hoped the lattes weren't going cold. "The notes from every meeting are emailed to every committee member. You received a copy. You never replied with any objections." She drew in a deep breath, but it only served to make her throat close against the cold. "Let's discuss this further at the meeting tonight," she croaked.

"Oh, we will." Fern whirled on her practical black pumps and stalked toward Jeremiah's.

LuAnn hurried to her car and reached inside to place the lattes in the cupholders. She slipped into the driver's seat, shut the door, and turned on the car, willing the heater to start immediately. Then she took a deep breath and closed her eyes. The confrontation was unexpected, even from acerbic Fern McPherson.

When the original chairwoman of the Marietta Christmas in History House Tour had delivered her baby two months early, the committee had gone into a semi-meltdown, and several of the stronger personalities threatened to derail the camaraderie that the group had enjoyed up to that point. LuAnn had been chosen to fill in as chairwoman by anonymous vote, but she did so reluctantly. The vote hadn't been unanimous, and the confrontation with Fern was a reminder of that fact.

LuAnn bowed her head. *Father, please help me handle this situation. I don't understand why Fern is so upset.*

She reached for the gearshift just as her phone buzzed with a text notification. She pulled it from her purse. It was from Jerri.

We're going to be on time—any minute.

On my way, LuAnn texted. *Picked up a plain latte for you and a breakfast wrap.*

Perfect. See you shortly. Can't wait.

LuAnn put her car in DRIVE and headed up the road, quickly covering the scant mile from Jeremiah's to the bus station. As she drove, her anticipation over seeing Jerri grew. LuAnn hadn't seen her old student in years. They'd communicated intermittently, mostly through social media. Because Jerri's sister Michele lived in Marietta, they'd anticipated seeing each other at some point. Now the time had arrived. But there was one niggling question in the back of LuAnn's mind—why had Jerri asked LuAnn to pick her up rather than ask her sister?

The bus arrived just as LuAnn parked. She exited her car to wait. When the willowy woman stepped down the bus stairs, LuAnn felt unexpected tears in her eyes. Jerri looked different from the thin, intense girl who had walked into LuAnn's classroom so long ago, yet LuAnn would have known her anywhere. She remembered Jerri's brash, even abrasive personality, the result of insecurities brought on by the death of her father and a mother who spiraled into drug abuse after her sister was born. Making matters worse, Jerri's mother ended up in prison, leaving her daughters to finish high school while they lived with their grandmother.

"Miss Sherrill!" Jerri's voice could have been heard a block away. LuAnn smiled. That hadn't changed either. Jerri hurtled toward LuAnn, arms outstretched, ignoring her suitcase that had been unloaded from the bus.

LuAnn barely remained standing, surprised by the intensity of the greeting, especially since Jerri didn't like hugs. "I'm LuAnn now, remember?" Her words were muffled in Jerri's coat-clad shoulder.

"I didn't realize just how glad I'd be to see you," Jerri murmured into LuAnn's neck before she took a step backward. "And I still don't hug people, so that was weird."

LuAnn smiled even while she choked back tears. "It's certainly a greeting I'll never forget. But you'd better go get your suitcase before someone else claims it." She pointed behind Jerri.

"Yes, ma'am." Jerri's laugh lingered in the air as she retrieved her bag.

When they'd settled into LuAnn's still running car, they grinned at each other. Jerri's coffee-colored skin and dark eyes sparkled with life, despite deep circles under them.

"Latte?" LuAnn held up Jerri's cup. "It might be lukewarm, but it's caffeine. And here's your breakfast wrap."

Jerri took both, laid the wrap on a napkin in her lap, and sipped the latte. "So good." She sighed and looked at LuAnn. "I remember the first time you brought me a hot drink—hot chocolate."

"I remember," LuAnn said softly.

"Then you got permission for me to study in your class-room after school."

"So I did." Memories flooded LuAnn's mind, making her feel weepy in a good way. She hoped she wouldn't spend the whole of Jerri's visit on the verge of sentimental blubbering. "And look at you now, working on your doctoral dissertation. You've come such a long way."

"I owe a lot of that to you, teaching me how to concentrate and study. Here's hoping I do you proud." Jerri lifted her drink.

"I'm sure you will." LuAnn lifted her latte, and they tapped the tops of their cups.

"I was sorry to hear of your grandmother's passing," LuAnn said. "I would have come to the funeral."

"I know you would have." Jerri picked at the paper around the breakfast wrap. "I didn't feel like I could ask you since I hadn't remained in real close contact with you. Besides, it was just a tiny affair at her church."

"I would have come, no matter what."

"I know."

LuAnn sipped her drink. They hadn't moved from the parking lot, but she didn't mind. She wasn't in a hurry.

"I miss Granny." Jerri pulled the paper from one end of the breakfast wrap and took a bite.

"She always did her best by you."

Jerri nodded and chewed. "She did. I appreciated that more as I got older." She paused, and her lower lip trembled. "Her death was a loss, for sure. But as I was cleaning out her attic, I found the papers that led to the research I'm doing for my dissertation. It was as if she left me one last gift. I can't wait to show you. It's cool. I think it's proof that one of my relatives came through Ohio on the Underground Railroad."

"And we can help you find more information." LuAnn put her latte in the cupholder and faced Jerri. "I'm curious about why you didn't have Michele come and pick you up."

Jerri put her wrap down. "I figured you'd ask me that. I'm embarrassed to say that I wanted you with me when I see her. We haven't been on the best of terms. We talk on the phone, but it's awkward and superficial."

"Does she know you've arrived?"

Jerri looked at her phone, forehead wrinkled. "I texted her and then tried to call her when the bus arrived in Marietta, but she's not answering. She might still be at work. She had one job scheduled for early this morning." Jerri glanced at LuAnn. "If she's not at home yet, she said her neighbor has a key. I'll get that, and maybe you and I could talk for a while until she arrives?"

"Of course. I set aside the whole morning for you." LuAnn put the car in Drive and headed out of the parking lot.

"Thank you." Jerri smiled, but tension pinched her mouth and eyes.

"You look tired. It's a long trip from Georgia."

"It is, but it's not the trip. I managed to sleep, thanks to earplugs, but I'm worried about Michele. She wanted me to come as soon as possible. When she called me last week, she sounded nervous."

"You mentioned that when we talked. She had some concerns about her job?"

"Yes, but then two hours ago, she called me to make sure I was really on my way. She sounded scared. And now she won't answer the phone."

LuAnn frowned. "That is odd."

"I'm torn between concern and irritation." Jerri clenched her fists. "Here I am, making a last-minute trip that I wanted to take next spring, traveling on a bus overnight because I didn't want to deal with the airports this time of year, all because she begged me to come. And she isn't answering my calls or texts. I would have thought she'd be waiting for me. Unless something is wrong."

"Perhaps she's just so excited you're coming that she forgot to turn her ringer on. Let's go find her. She's still on Charles Street, right?"

"Yes, she is."

LuAnn turned onto the Byway, driving past Marietta College and True Value Hardware.

Jerri ate more of her breakfast then faced LuAnn. "I call Michele every week, mostly because my grandmother used to make me, and now I do it out of habit. The conversations are short. 'I'm fine. You're fine. I like my dog.' It's as if she doesn't want me to be part of her life. Do you remember that she used to be into some drug stuff?"

LuAnn nodded.

"As far as I can tell, she's been totally clean for a couple of years now. She has new friends. She even started going to church." Jerri sighed. "For some reason I've always brought out the worst in her. Sibling rivalry, maybe? Like she had to compete with me."

"I remember some of the issues you two had when you were young."

"Apparently the issues haven't changed, but the way we handle them has. We no longer fight. She avoids talking to me about anything important. And I just try not to think about her much."

LuAnn ached at the bitterness and hurt in Jerri's voice.

"Anyway, I was surprised when she suddenly called me out of the blue and said something was wrong. She needed me. She was afraid of something. It reminded me of the past when she was scared as a little kid." Jerri's voice sank to a whisper. "I really had no choice. I had to come."

Jerri, always the rescuer of her little sister. LuAnn reached over and patted her arm. "I did try to contact Michele after I moved here, but she didn't seem interested in seeing me. That was over a year ago. I didn't want to be a pest, so I haven't contacted her for a while."

"Probably because she associates you with me and doesn't want to get close."

LuAnn glanced at Jerri. "That could be. But maybe this visit will be the very thing that brings the two of you together. After all, it is the Christmas season. Jesus' birth. God's mercy in the flesh. His plan to reconcile humans to Himself."

"Yeah, I guess."

LuAnn felt a wall go up between them. Jerri turned her head to stare out the window. The skepticism she'd had as a teenager about the things of God hadn't changed. The little girl who had gone to Sunday school and church with her grandmother had disappeared somewhere underneath the hard shell of a struggling adult.

Jerri finished her breakfast wrap and crumpled the paper just as LuAnn rounded the corner onto Charles Street. She almost skidded to a stop. Red lights blinked ahead of her.

Jerri leaned forward. "Is that an ambulance?"

"Yes, it is." LuAnn saw someone being loaded onto a stretcher.

"That's Michele's house! Is that her they're loading up?" Jerri jammed her latte in the cupholder.

"It might be. I'll park so we can get out." LuAnn pulled along the side of the road.

Jerri jumped from the car and ran toward the scene. LuAnn followed.

A small crowd had gathered in front of a small blue Cape Cod, clutching their coats close to their bodies, breath coming out in steam.

Jerri shoved past them. "That's my sister! What's happened?"

An older short woman, whose full head of spiky dyed red hair stuck out in all directions, moved closer to Jerri. "Michele was upset. I yelled out the door for her to be careful, but she wasn't paying attention. Down she went on a patch of ice. I told the county they needed to do something about it." The woman pointed to ice on the cracked cement sidewalk.

A tiny, scrawny terrier mix, leash dangling on the ground, panted and whined next to the stretcher. Jerri tried to get closer, but a medic stopped her.

"Ma'am, we have to get her to the hospital. She's had a nasty knock to her head."

"But she's my sister!" Jerri cried. "I want to go with you. I'm her only family here."

"Sorry, ma'am. No can do. I sympathize, but I need you to please step aside and let us do our job."

LuAnn touched Jerri's shoulder to prevent her from causing a scene. "I'll take you. We'll follow them, okay?"

Jerri's nostrils flared. "Yes, okay."

The back door to the ambulance slammed shut. The paramedics jumped in the front, and the vehicle drove away, lights flashing, siren wailing.

The terrier barked and whined. LuAnn grabbed the leash just in time to keep the little dog from following. The crowd dispersed, heading back to their houses.

"What do I do about the dog?" Jerri glanced around in a panic. "She loves that dog."

The red-haired woman stepped up and reached out for the leash. "I'll watch her for you. I'm Mrs. Brewster. I live just next door." She pointed to a house that was a mirror-image of Michele's. "I take it you're Jerri?"

Jerri nodded.

"Michele told me you were coming."

LuAnn handed the leash to Mrs. Brewster. "Thank you."

A tall man wearing shiny cowboy boots joined her. "I can always walk him if Mrs. Brewster can't."

"Thank you both," LuAnn said.

"Um, okay." Jerri glanced at the two of them with confusion and turned to LuAnn. "All I really care about right now is getting to the hospital. Let's go."

A NOTE FROM THE EDITORS

We hope you enjoy Secrets of Wayfarers Inn, created by the Books and Inspirational Media Division of Guideposts, a nonprofit organization that touches millions of lives every day through products and services that inspire, encourage, help you grow in your faith, and celebrate God's love in every aspect of your daily life.

Thank you for making a difference with your purchase of this book, which helps fund our many outreach programs to military personnel, prisons, hospitals, nursing homes, and educational institutions. To learn more, visit Guideposts Foundation.org.

We also maintain many useful and uplifting online resources. Visit Guideposts.org to read true stories of hope and inspiration, access OurPrayer network, sign up for free newsletters, download free e-books, join our Facebook community, and follow our stimulating blogs.

To learn about other Guideposts publications, including the best-selling devotional *Daily Guideposts*, go to ShopGuideposts .org, call (800) 932-2145, or write to Guideposts, PO Box 5815, Harlan, Iowa 51593.

Sign up for the Guideposts Fiction Newsletter

and stay up to date on the books you love!

You'll get sneak peeks of new releases, recommendations from other Guideposts readers, and special offers just for you . . . ***and it's FREE!***

Just go to Guideposts.org/Newsletters today to sign up.

Guideposts®

Visit Guideposts.org/Shop
or call (800) 932-2145

Find more inspiring fiction in these best-loved Guideposts series!

Tearoom Mysteries Series

Mix one stately Victorian home, a charming lakeside town in Maine, and two adventurous cousins with a passion for tea and hospitality. Add a large scoop of intriguing mystery and sprinkle generously with faith, family, and friends, and you have the recipe for *Tearoom Mysteries*.

Sugarcreek Amish Mysteries

Be intrigued by the suspense and joyful "aha" moments in these delightful stories. Each book in the series brings together two women of vastly different backgrounds and traditions, who realize there's much more to the "simple life" than meets the eye.

Mysteries of Martha's Vineyard

What does Priscilla Latham Grant, a Kansas farm girl know about hidden treasure and rising tides, maritime history and local isle lore? Not much—but to save her lighthouse and family reputation, she better learn quickly!

Mysteries of Silver Peak

Escape to the historic mining town of Silver Peak, Colorado, and discover how one woman's love of antiques helps her solve mysteries buried deep in the town's checkered past.

To learn more about these books, visit Guideposts.org/Shop